POSTSCRIPT

ANNE BARWELL

KEDGETOWN, BOOK 1

Tales from a magical bookshop.

ISBN: 978-1-99-116212-0 (epub)
ISBN: 978-1-99-116213-7 (print)

AUTHOR'S NOTE

Kedgetown is a fictional town in the Wairarapa region of Wellington.

ALSO BY ANNE BARWELL

Slow Dreaming

On Wings of Song

Prelude to Love

The Sleepless City

Shades of Sepia

Electric Candle by Elizabeth Noble

Family and Reflection

Shifting Chaos by Elizabeth Noble

Pōneke Shadows

Double Exposure

Echoes Rising

Shadowboxing

Winter Duet

Comes a Horseman

CO-WRITTEN WITH LOU SYLVRE

Magic in the Isles

The Harp and the Sea

In memory of Kaylee, my beloved cat of 18 years, who passed away in 2022. I wouldn't be surprised if Postscript gets a ghost kitty at some point.

ACKNOWLEDGMENTS

To Elizabeth, my shared universe partner in crime, who alpha and beta read, brainstormed, and was a huge support throughout.

To Angela for beta reading.

To Fiona who wanted a character in a romance book named after her.

To my writing and reading communities for your support and friends, in particular RWNZ, and my Facebook group Anne's Books and Brews. A special thanks to the New Zealand Rainbow Romance Writers group—you guys rock.

T.L Bland for her wonderful cover art.

Penny for editing.

Lissa and Maryann for proofing.

To my family. Love you.

CHAPTER ONE

Mason Chynoweth hadn't dared risk using his psychic ability, but something in this old house spoke to him. He'd found nowhere he thought of as home until now.

The presence he'd sensed wrapped him with a gentle warmth like an old favourite blanket.

He yawned.

The woman behind him chuckled. "You feel it, then? I thought you'd be one of those we're looking for."

Mason frowned. What was she on about? His shoulders stiffened, tension spreading through him. "I'm tired, that's all." He wouldn't give her any hints he was anything but boringly average.

"Of course you are." Annalise Whitaker smiled. "And where are my manners? You've had a long drive here, and now you've seen the house, you will want to get settled. She's not habitable at present." Annalise rested a hand on one of the dust-cloth-covered pieces of furniture, and fine particles filled the air.

"She?"

"The shop, of course." While Annalise was nice enough

and welcoming, she gave off a distinctively weird vibe he couldn't quite put his finger on.

Not that he was one to talk where weirdness was concerned. At least he tried not to be.

"It's a house, not a shop." Mason frowned. The papers he'd received from his lawyer telling him about his inheritance had described the house as a lovely character villa. He'd always loved those.

"Ah yes, sometimes it is." Annalise gestured to Mason's backpack. "If you collect your bag, I can show you your room and get you settled." She ran the local B&B and had known Lewis, so she offered to show Mason the house. "It will be dark soon, and you'll want to take a better look in the light."

"How long has the house been shut up?" Mason stepped past her onto the street, careful not to touch anything, despite wearing gloves.

Lewis's death had never been documented. But given his younger sister had passed away five years ago, a couple of months before her hundredth birthday, he had to have been gone for at least a decade. The lawyer handling the estate was acting on the instructions of Lewis's accountant, Victor Rochford.

"Beginning of February." Annalise used an old-fashioned key to lock the front door and handed it to Mason. "You need to keep this safe."

"There's no spare?" Not that he had any intention of losing the key, but he had to ask anyway. "What about whoever has been renting the house since Lewis's death? They must have returned theirs when they moved out, right?"

"The house hasn't been rented out, so you don't need to worry about someone else still having access to it. She is very particular about that." Annalise sounded businesslike all of a sudden. "We're still waiting on the other key, but I don't think he'll be long now you're here."

"He? But didn't you say the house has been empty since February?" Mason frowned. "It must have been rented out before then, though. Lewis…." His head hurt trying to fill in gaps that made no sense. "Do you know why I got the house and not Fiona? She's a year older than me."

"Fiona has her own path, dear, although I'm sure hers will cross with yours at some point." Annalise smiled again, and her expression softened. "Soon enough," she added, as though speaking to someone behind Mason.

He turned, but no one was there.

"Lewis called in briefly to see Nana after he returned from the war, and that was the last any of the family saw him." One of the reasons Mason had come to Kedgetown was to learn more about their mysterious great-great uncle. "We didn't know what had happened to him until my sister met him here last Christmas. And then he left me the house."

Fiona had never said why she'd visited Kedgetown, but then her ability gave her opportunities his didn't.

Lewis Newman had answered an ad in the local paper for a position at Kedgetown's post office. He had only been there about a year before WWII had broken out. Like so many others, he'd shipped out to fight in Europe. Any information after that was patchy at best. Fiona had asked her friend, Ennis, who worked at Archives New Zealand, to find out more, but he'd had little luck. Lewis arrived back in Kedgetown in 1945, suffering from what was now known as PTSD, and their family lost contact with him soon afterwards.

Until Fiona's encounter, which Mason suspected wasn't entirely down to chance.

"Poor boy. It took a lot of TLC and love for him to find himself again after his wartime experiences in Europe."

Annalise shook her head. "War is a terrible thing. You're never the same afterwards. That's why she's so important."

"The house?" Mason frowned. What was he missing? Weren't boats referred to as she? Not houses.

Annalise nodded, but before she could offer more of an explanation, a man about Mason's age ran down the street towards them. Mason instinctively stepped to one side to let him pass. The man skidded to a halt and pulled Annalise into a hug.

"You haven't changed a bit, Aunty A," he said after she broke the hug.

"It's nice to see you too, Elijah." Annalise grinned and ruffled the top of Elijah's head. "We have a visitor, so I'll be needing your help to ensure Mason here feels at home."

Elijah spun around to face Mason. "Hi! I'm Elijah Whitaker. Nice to meet you." At over six feet, he was taller than Mason by a good three inches and built like a bear. Red whiskers covered Elijah's chin, a darker auburn contrasting the almost carrot colour of the hair peeking out the sides of his beanie. Bright blue eyes were coupled with a huge grin. Elijah gave the impression of someone who grabbed life and lived it to the fullest.

"Mason Chynoweth." Mason neatly sidestepped Elijah's outstretched hand and made a show of rearranging his backpack.

Elijah lowered his hand, a dark expression crossing his face. An awkward silence lingered between them. "I'm sorry," he mumbled. "I didn't mean to—"

"It's not you," Mason said quickly, not wanting to upset someone he'd just met. "I don't—"

Annalise called out to them from a few metres down the road. "Hurry up, boys. We don't want to be late for dinner."

∼

Elijah wrapped his fingers around a cup of lemon ginger tea. His stomach rumbled in appreciation of the wonderful smell of the rich meat and vegetable casserole almost ready to come out of the oven.

He smiled, watching Annalise and Rilla talk in low voices on the other side of the kitchen. He heard his name and Mason's mentioned a couple of times and shook his head. Annalise had been at him for a while to stay with them, and her hints he might find a lovely young man to settle down with weren't subtle. She meant well, but he liked the Canterbury region and never found anyone worth moving for.

Rilla chuckled, brushed a strand of blonde hair behind one ear, and brushed her lips against Annalise's cheek. "Annalise has talked for weeks about you coming home. It's lovely to see you again. It's been a while, hasn't it?"

He wished he could hug her and wondered, not for the first time, how his aunt coped with having the woman she loved so close, yet not. "A couple of years, at least."

Elijah had moved to Christchurch with his parents the year before he started high school. Most of his childhood friends had moved away and were scattered around the country. With the town's size, there weren't many jobs, although some of the original residents came home to retire. Annalise and Rilla had taken over the B&B in the 1940s, although Rilla hadn't gone far since she'd passed away forty years before. Elijah wasn't sure what she was tied to, and it was considered impolite to ask, so he didn't.

"I hope you're staying with us this time." Rilla lowered her voice, although Annalise would still be able to hear her. "She misses you. We both do."

"For a few months, but I can't promise anything past that." Elijah shrugged. "Work is busy. Plenty of construction since the quakes."

"There are construction companies up here looking for

good workers, too," Rilla said. "You'd be closer, and we'd see you more often."

"Rilla," Annalise chastised. "He'll work out where he's meant to be soon enough. Relax and let it happen."

Rilla giggled, sounding like the young woman she appeared rather than the age she'd been when she'd died. "You know I can never resist giving a little nudge, my love. After all those years of helping people find their happy ever afters, I want one for our Elijah too."

"You two are as bad as each other," Elijah teased, although privately, he loved they cared enough to want him to be happy. Seeing them together reminded him of what he was missing. It was a decade since he and Sinclair had broken up, although their relationship hadn't been great for most of the two years they'd been together. Elijah had tried, but in the end, the secret he couldn't share was the final nail in the coffin. He'd fled to Kedgetown, bared his soul to his aunts, returned to Christchurch and kept himself busy with work.

His parents were very traditional. His mother was relieved the relationship hadn't worked out. His father… never exactly shared his thoughts on the matter, but the looks Elijah received said it all. He was lucky they'd finally left him alone and given up hounding him to find a job in Wellington with the Waylands. He wasn't interested in real estate, and a change in scenery and occupation wasn't what he needed either.

"Mason seems a nice boy," Rilla said.

"He's not one of us," Elijah pointed out. "I can't go through that again." He paused. "However nice he is."

What was up with Mason anyway? His reaction to Elijah's proffered hand was… unusual. Sure, some people weren't touchy-feely, but Mason didn't seem merely reluctant to shake hands. He looked terrified.

As if on cue, Mason poked his head into the kitchen.

"Whatever you're cooking smells wonderful." He hesitated. "I don't want to intrude on your family reunion, though, so I'm happy to eat in my room."

"Nonsense," Annalise said briskly. "You're our only visitor, apart from Elijah, so of course, you can join us for dinner." She frowned. "I hope you're not vegetarian. Sorry, I should have checked."

Mason slid into the empty chair opposite Elijah. His gaze lingered on Elijah, and then he turned away, a slow flush creeping over his face. "I'll eat anything. As long as you don't have any olives hiding in there. I'm not fond of those."

"No olives. Promise." Annalise spooned a generous portion of food onto three plates, laid them on the table, and took the other seat, "I never cook with them when Elijah's here. He hates them, and besides, they don't go with this recipe."

Rilla settled herself on the barstool and winked at Elijah. "See, something in common already."

Elijah sighed. "Not going there, Aunty."

Annalise moved the conversation on before Mason could ask what the hell Elijah was on about. "It's warm in here. You'll be okay to take your gloves off to eat."

"Umm…." Mason shot her a panicked look. "I… guess." He peeled off his lightweight woollen gloves and shoved them in his pocket. He picked up a fork and then let out a breath. "I'm sorry. I… I spend a lot of time on my own. I don't mean to be rude."

"No need to apologise," Elijah said quickly before Annalise could hijack the conversation.

Mason rewarded him with a smile and started to eat. He'd soon put on weight if he stayed at Moonside B&B for any length of time. Not that he needed to. As he'd adjusted his backpack earlier, Elijah had spotted a flat stomach and a hint of muscle when Mason's shirt and jumper had ridden up.

Mason was a striking man with his blond, almost white hair offset by dark eyes. Was his hair colour natural?

Unfortunately, that was something Elijah was probably never going to find out.

"Mason's inherited the old house on Main Street," Annalise said, a smile tugging at her lips. "There's a lot of work to do there as the house has been closed up since February. That's four months of dust to get rid of and all sorts of hidden treasures to find."

"I don't remember ever seeing anyone living there." Elijah frowned at the wording Annalise had used. She always carefully chose the information she imparted.

"It was a completely different place in the three months before then," Rilla said. "I enjoyed meeting up with those two young men again. They always make me feel so welcome."

Mason frowned. "But I thought you said—"

"Kedgetown has always prided itself on being welcoming." Annalise interrupted as though Mason hadn't spoken. "It's part of its magic."

Elijah choked on his mouthful of gravy. Mason was a stranger. They didn't talk about the town or its history in front of anyone who hadn't grown up here. Or make comments that might lead to awkward questions. If Mason decided to make his home here and settle in the old house, Elijah definitely would not stick around. He'd had enough of lying about who he was.

"Are you okay?" Mason put down his fork, concerned.

"Yeah." Elijah shot his aunts a glare. What were they up to? He didn't believe their innocent expressions for a moment. "Went down the wrong way."

"What do you do for a living, Mason, dear?" Annalise moved the conversation along.

"I work in IT. Data entry mainly." Mason shrugged. "It's not very exciting, but it pays the bills, and I can do it from home." He paused. "Which at the moment is Invercargill, but if the house pans out, it *is* something I could do from anywhere."

"Mason likes the house so far, and I suspect it's mutual. But, as I said, there's a lot of work to do first." Annalise got up from the table, retrieved the casserole dish, and placed it between Mason and Elijah. "You boys still look hungry. Help yourselves if you want more."

"Thanks." Elijah spooned more onto his plate. He'd forgotten what a good cook his aunt was. "Is your family in Invercargill?"

"My parents are, but the rest of my family live on the West Coast. My sister lives in Greytown, so she's only an hour away, although she's only visited Kedgetown once."

Mason waited until Elijah had finished, then reached for the serving spoon at the same time Elijah handed it to him. Their fingers brushed. Mason went rigid. All colour drained from his face. He looked like he'd seen a ghost.

Elijah glanced at Rilla, who was behind Mason. She shrugged.

The serving spoon clattered to the table.

"Mason?" Elijah pushed back his chair to go to Mason.

Annalise laid a warning hand on Elijah's arm. "Give him a moment to come back to us. Perhaps a cup of tea would be a good idea. For later."

A moment later, Mason gasped for breath. "I saw… what…." He glanced around the table.

"It's a very old serving spoon," Annalise said. "With a lot of history. It was a wedding present from an old friend. I'm not exactly sure of its origins."

Mason relaxed a little. "I'm sorry I don't mean to be rude." He massaged his temples. "I have a… headache. Thank you for the lovely meal. I'll see you in the morning."

He stood and bolted, footsteps loud against the wood of the stairs to his bedroom. He closed the door behind him.

Elijah stared after him. "What the hell?"

"Tea, I'm thinking." Rilla sounded thoughtful and more than a little smug. "The special one you used to make for me."

"Definitely." Annalise's eyes glowed gold, and she smiled. "I suspected as much after we met his sister last Christmas, but this is even better than we thought."

"Huh?" Elijah glanced from one aunty to the other. "What are you up to?"

"Us? We're looking after our visitors like any good host would." Annalise walked over to the kitchen to put the kettle on. "Help me clean up, will you? And then you can take Mason a nice cup of tea."

CHAPTER TWO

Mason curled up on the floor in the corner of his room and buried his head in his hands. Shit, how could he have been so stupid? His head thumped with the beginning of a stress headache, and he took several deep breaths to calm his racing heart.

In out. In out.

Nana had said focusing on his breathing would help. It usually did.

Totally not the way to impress a guy he'd recently met. Not that dating was an option. Mason had tried that one before, and it ended in disaster. Jack was caring and understanding at first, and Mason had seriously thought about breaking his Nana's rule about not telling anyone their family secret.

Fiona had called Jack a fuckwit and offered to go around and tell him what she thought, but luckily Mason stopped her in time. Jack's reaction wasn't unexpected, and he'd put up with a lot of Mason's bullshit before calling it quits. Fortunately, his ability rarely had problems with people, and only objects pinged his psi radar.

If he'd been careful, he might have been able to trust Jack and ease him into the idea that his boyfriend had weird-arse powers. Instead, Mason had a major meltdown after brushing against, of all things, an old umbrella stand at a café. He should have stuck to his guns rather than let Jack convince him to try the new place around the corner.

Instead, he'd frozen as images from the past bombarded him.

A glimpse of a city decades ago. Old-fashioned cars in the street. Gunshots. Blood. A man falling to the ground, his vision shrinking into blackness while a woman sobbed.

Jack's concern had quickly morphed into fear as Mason had clung to him, shaking, talking nonsense.

He couldn't explain. Not when it would have made him sound crazier than he already did.

The stand had originated from London and come to New Zealand on a ship with someone immigrating after the last world war. The café owner's grandmother had lost her husband in a robbery gone wrong. He'd made the stand for her, so she hadn't wanted to part with it.

The explanation came later when Mason had wanted some context for his experience and rang the café to apologise.

Not all his visions were that bad, but he couldn't take the risk again. He retreated, worked from home, and barely ventured outside his front door. He wore gloves when he went out and kept his distance from anything that could set off another vision.

Then he'd collected pizza from the delivery guy. Their fingers brushed, and Mason had been blindsided by touching someone rather than something for the first time ever.

Not only that, but Jack had seen Mason's reaction to that one, too.

Jack had offered to get him help, but that would have meant coming clean about everything, which wasn't an option. So, Mason had cut all ties. Promised he'd get help.

More lies.

Telling someone outside the family was too dangerous, and he couldn't risk exposing himself and, by extension, the people he cared about. Trusting a friend might have worked for Fiona, but she'd been lucky enough to find someone else with *an ability* to confide in.

Was that why Lewis had disappeared? Had he told someone he shouldn't? Fiona had said nothing about how or when he'd died, only that she'd met him last Christmas.

Mason sighed. He couldn't afford to get stuck in his own past. Not when he was trying to deal with someone else's.

Had this vision been triggered by Elijah or the serving spoon? The hell if Mason knew. Maybe he was finally losing the plot? The vision was very similar to what he'd picked up from the pizza guy. A full moon and howling that sent shivers up his spine.

He forced himself to stand, and the room spun.

Wonderful.

Strong arms caught him and helped him over to the loveseat by the window.

"You okay?" Elijah studied him.

"Yeah, thanks. Sorry I didn't hear you come in." Mason blinked up at Elijah's concerned gaze.

"I knocked, and you didn't answer." Elijah retrieved a mug of steaming liquid from the bedside table. "I heard… noises… and saw you fall." He handed Mason the mug and sat next to him on the sofa. "I could call the doctor if you'd like. Scott's a good guy, and he's seen all sorts of stuff, so he—"

"Wouldn't judge?" Mason heard the bitterness in his response and cringed. Elijah was only trying to help. "I hope your aunt isn't too concerned. I get… this sometimes. I'll be fine." The spoon was obviously the culprit, as Elijah's touch now wasn't triggering another vision. Mason started to relax. He missed sitting like this and talking to someone. Since the pizza delivery guy incident, Mason had taken to being cautious around people too. Discovering the lightweight merino gloves he now favoured was a godsend.

Warmth spread through his jeans from where their knees touched. Elijah must have been sitting on top of a heater. Mason moved closer, soaking it up while he still could.

"She sent me up with the tea." Elijah gestured to the mug. "It's herbal, and she said it would help." He hesitated before continuing. "Aunty Rilla used to get… headaches… like yours. This always helped her. Don't ask me what's in it, though, as I have no clue." He chuckled. "I've found it's better not to ask too many questions about Annalise's teas."

Mason took a tentative sip. Peppermint. Maybe lemon. And a couple of other things he couldn't identify. "Tastes good," he murmured.

"You have more colour in your face than you did a few minutes ago." Elijah sounded relieved though he still watched Mason like a hawk.

"I usually start to feel better about half an hour after the… headaches," Mason reassured him. His brain caught up with what Elijah had said about the tea. "Who's Rilla?" He'd only seen one of Elijah's aunts, although something else itched at the edge of his senses. Though considering he'd just had a vision, that wasn't unexpected.

"Annalise's wife." Elijah smiled. "I spent a lot of time over here with them before we moved away. We're close. Closer than I am to my own parents, always have been."

"Family's important. Fiona and I spend a lot of time with my grandparents and go to see them when we can." Mason took another sip of the tea. He'd already drunk half of it without realising. "This is very good."

"So, the old house?" Elijah sounded intrigued. "I haven't returned to Kedgetown much over the last twe—few years. It's been deserted for as long as I can remember." He frowned. "I think it used to be a bookshop, but I could be wrong. Or perhaps I'm mixing the house up with a bookshop somewhere else."

"Have you been inside? I'd love to get some insight into the place that isn't your aunt's." Mason inhaled the tea. It smelled amazing, too. "Not that your aunt's opinion isn't welcome," he added hurriedly.

Elijah chuckled. "Aunty A can be a bit overwhelming when she gets going. She and Rilla together. I swear they're a force to be reckoned with." He paused. "I used to peer inside the house when I was a kid. My friends and I used to wipe ice from the windows during winter. For some reason, the building always reminded me of something sleeping, like it was hibernating, waiting for the right person to wake it up. Sorry, that sounds crazy."

"No, that makes perfect sense. I got that vibe from it, too. What about the bookshop?"

The house could easily be turned into a bookshop. Not that he'd do that. He shivered. Books came with history, and that was dangerous for someone like him.

"Perhaps it was a bookshop once?" Mason wondered. "Nana said Lewis loved books." Could that be a clue? "Maybe he had a bookshop on the premises." Reality caught up with him. "But you said you remembered a bookshop when you were a kid, so that was what… twenty years ago, if that? Lewis was here decades ago, although he must have come back since then as he still owned the house." Mason took a moment to consider. "Yeah, that makes more sense. Your aunty knew him more recently from the way she talked about him, and she would have been a child when he first moved here."

"I remember the bookshop at Christmas," Elijah confirmed. "Every year, the aunties would take me to choose a book to read over the summer holidays." He shrugged. "I've only been back in town during winter since, and I don't remember seeing it then. My memories of it are hazy. A couple of guys ran the shop, but I don't remember their names."

"Could it have been at the house?"

"Maybe… I don't know." Elijah sighed. "Sorry, all I'm doing is muddying the waters. Lewis is your great-great-uncle?"

"One of the reasons I'm here is to learn more about him and why he left me the house. My great-grandmother was his sister, although we called her Nana, and my grandmother is Gran. Granddad was Nana's eldest, but Dad has an older brother, so why not leave it to one of my cousins?" Not all his cousins were psi. Could that be it? "Fiona would be a better choice. She's older than me too."

"Are you going to keep the house?"

"I don't know." Mason placed the cup carefully on the floor by the couch. It hadn't triggered a vision either, so that was a start. But then, not everything did. He'd have a run of good luck, then suddenly be hit by something that more than made up for it.

Elijah chewed on his bottom lip. "I'm here for a couple of months, maybe longer. I could give you a hand to sort through it if you like." He ducked his head. "Or not. Completely up to you."

"I'd like that." Mason hadn't felt relaxed around someone who wasn't family for such a long time.

"Great." Elijah rewarded Mason with a grin. "It's nice out tonight. I could show you around the town if you like."

"We could peer in shop windows." Mason liked the sound of that. He could survey what would be his home for the next few weeks without mixing with a lot of people. "I need a shower first, though, as I've been travelling all day. Meet you downstairs in half an hour?"

"Sure." Elijah reached for Mason's cup.

"Don't worry about that. I'll bring it down with me on the way out. That way, I can say thanks to Annalise. Maybe meet Rilla if she's home by then."

Elijah froze. "Oh shit. I haven't told you."

"Told me what?"

"You won't be meeting her, sorry." Elijah stood. He seemed nervous. "I was so busy talking about the past and my memories that I... Aunty Rilla passed away forty years ago." He smiled softly. "Although some days it feels like she's still with us, you know? Gone, but not forgotten, yeah?"

"Not always gone, either," Mason added once Elijah was safely out of earshot. He had a medium in the family, so he knew that better than most.

Elijah couldn't help smiling at Mason coming down the stairs. He was wrapped up in a scarf, gloves, and an adorable knitted beanie with a penguin on it. "Being from Invercargill, I thought you'd be used to the cold," he teased.

"That doesn't mean I have to like it." Mason straightened his beanie. "Besides, it's the last thing Nana knitted for me before she died, so it's like she's still with me when I wear it."

"I think it's adorable." Elijah's mouth twitched. The words had slipped out before he'd had the chance to censor them. Not that his brain-to-mouth filter was great at the best of times. Hopefully, Mason hadn't meant literally that his nana was with him. One matchmaking ghost was more than enough.

Mason's face reddened, and then he poked out his tongue. "Smart arse."

"It's important to dress warmly outside," Annalise called from the kitchen. "I'll have supper ready for you boys when you get home."

"Yes, Aunty A." Elijah opened the door and ushered Mason out into the garden before Rilla could add her two cents worth.

"I'm not usually into cutesy hats." Mason obviously needed to explain.

"Sorry I teased you. That was totally out of line." Elijah glanced up at the sky. The full moon was a couple of weeks away. How the hell was he going to convince Mason to stay in his room? Annalise usually didn't take bookings around that time of the month. What had she been thinking? He shoved his hands in his pockets, risked a look at Mason, and waited for his response.

"I don't mind." Mason smiled softly, and then the expression flattened as though he had second thoughts.

"Okay." Elijah made a mental note not to flirt with the sexy new guy in town. Mason wouldn't be staying, and even if he decided to, they wouldn't have a future. Kedgetown might be one big happy family with its relaxed attitude to most rules, but revealing who he was to a human still wasn't allowed. "What do you want me to show you first?"

"There's only one main street, right?"

"Yeah, of shops, although the town is built around it, so we have a few streets of houses and others further out. Farms mainly, and a couple of orchards which are totally worth checking out in the summer fruit season."

"Let's start with the main street, then." Mason followed

Elijah out the front gate. "What's the best place to start? I read what I could about the town, but there's not much out there."

Moonrise was directly behind the old house, and the two properties, which were separated by a fence, backed onto each other.

"We have choices. There's a gate between us and your house, or we could walk around the block to Main Street and work our way from one end to the other."

"There's a gate?" Mason sounded surprised. "Could you show me that in daylight?"

"Sure. To be honest, the back of your section is so overgrown I'm not sure we could go through." Weird. Elijah hadn't remembered that gate until a couple of moments before he'd mentioned it. But that was Kedgetown for you. The town had a knack for showing you what you needed to know at the right time and not before. "So, left or right? We're right in the middle."

"Right," Mason decided. "You can tell me a bit about Kedgetown's history as we walk."

"Okay." Elijah racked his brain for the official spiel, the one he could share. "Not much to say, really. It's never had a big population, although we get a few tourists through in the summer. There's another B&B a couple of streets over and two pubs on the main street. Both offer rooms and meals."

"So, a population of about two thousand?"

Elijah chuckled. "Usually about half of that. Most of the kids don't stick around once they finish high school. It's easier to find a flat closer to uni or work, and there's not much of that locally, depending on the job you want to do. A few take the train into Wellington or Masterton in the other direction, but we mainly keep to ourselves. We're not on the train line, so the drive to the station adds to the commute."

"A commute's not a problem if you work from home," Mason noted.

"There's that." Elijah had a group of friends he went out with in Christchurch on pub crawls, but he didn't miss them in the weeks between seeing each other. He'd hooked up with a guy from the local pack since the Sinclair debacle but made a point of ghosting him at the first hint of anything serious. All Elijah wanted was a bit of fun, nothing else. "You're seriously thinking about staying?"

"Define seriously." Mason stepped back onto the road and studied the front of the bank as they rounded the corner. "Are all the businesses here in old houses?"

"Yep. And if it's a two-storey, the owners have their business downstairs and live above them." Elijah had forgotten how much he loved the old-fashioned décor of the town. "Mostly owned too. Not many rentals." The council was very choosy about who moved into town, despite its open-door policy to give haven to anyone in need.

Most of the humans in town possessed abilities that either wouldn't be welcome elsewhere or would put them at risk from those who might find out about them.

And then there was the surviving founder, and he was something no one would ever mention to an outsider like Mason.

"Interesting." Mason walked back to the footpath. "I love the street lights. They're wonderfully old-fashioned and remind me of Narnia."

"Me too! I loved those books." Elijah hadn't shown someone new around town for ages. His own delight in being here faded the longer he stayed away, but, as usual, after a few hours of being back, he felt like he'd never left.

"So this one's the dairy?" Mason glanced up the street and back again. "No supermarket?"

"No big retail chains allowed. It's part of the town policy.

If we want something that isn't available in town, we go further afield for it. Only an hour's drive to Greytown or Featherston, so it's not as though we don't have options. Doing that once a month or so, or ordering stuff online, isn't much of a hardship." Elijah moved the conversation on. "And this is our medical centre."

"Hi, Elijah." Scott Kelly waved from his rocking chair on the front porch. "And you must be Mason. The aunties told me you were coming."

Elijah rolled his eyes. Of course, they had. "Mason's first night, so I'm showing him around. Scott, Mason. Mason, Scott. Scott's our local GP."

"Nice to meet you, Mason." Scott tipped his hat to them. Although he looked like he was in his forties, he'd been in the town for as long as anyone could remember. "Elijah, tell your aunties that Wendy will call on them tomorrow."

"Will do." Elijah glanced at Mason, who wore a befuddled expression. How much had he seen? It wasn't like Scott to be careless around visitors. "Come on," he urged. "The temperature's dropping, and Aunty A will have hot cocoa waiting for us at home."

"Trick of the light," Mason mumbled. "Right?" His voice sounded strained. "And why would he say she'd be visiting both your aunties? You said your Aunt Rilla had passed away."

"Depends on what you think you saw." Elijah led Mason past his house to the bench seat in front of the Post Office. He deliberately didn't answer Mason's question about Rilla.

"Scott... his ears look weird. No pinna, just a hole."

"Do they?" Elijah narrowed his eyes. He wasn't sure what the aunties thought they were doing and who else was in on it, but he was going to have a word with them once Mason was safely out of earshot. "Maybe your headache is lingering a bit? Do you need an early night?"

"I'm fine." Mason hesitated. "Sorry, some days I think I'm losing the plot, you know? Perhaps I'm more tired than I thought. And don't think I didn't notice you didn't answer my question about your Aunt Rilla. Or are you trying to tell me the B&B is haunted?"

"Rilla would be one to stick around, that's for sure." Elijah kept his voice light, unsure whether Mason's willingness to believe in the supernatural was a good thing. "You've had a long day and a lot thrown at you." He gestured to the end of the street. "We can visit the park some other time. The church is over the road from it." He'd avoid the graveyard next door, as that was a whole other level of explanation.

"Presbyterian, Catholic, or something else?"

"Whatever you need." Elijah frowned, trying to remember if the last guy had run when he'd figured out who his parishioners were, or whether he was one of the few who stuck around. "We have a minister who lives in the manse behind it. At least, I think we still do. Anyway, Father Elard still visits once a month, more often if you ask him to. He's an old friend of the aunties." He'd presided over the ceremony when the aunties had married, although neither was Catholic. Back then, no human minister would marry two women, and the pack… they were even more backwards about one of their own marrying a human.

"Perhaps if you tell me about the rest of the street, and we can head back in a few." Mason massaged his temples.

"Sure." Elijah breathed a sigh of relief that Mason hadn't noticed Scott talking about aunties, plural, and his own slip in that regard. "One pub next to the Post Office, the other at the end of the street opposite the bank. The council offices are over the road."

"That building is much bigger than the rest," Mason noted.

"Noticed that too, huh?" Elijah shook his head. Although

they rarely had a visit from anyone from *that* council, they did turn up on occasion and expected to be treated like their opinion counted. The building, which doubled as the community house and library, helped to maintain that façade.

"What's that one?" Mason perked up. He stood and crossed the road to the bakery, completely ignoring the general store next to it. He seemed drawn to it, like a moth to a flame.

Elijah ran to keep up with him. "That's the bakery and definitely a place you must check out when it's open. Everything they make is amazing."

"There's something…." Mason wiped the window clear, leaving a space big enough for both of them to look through. His gloved hand came away wet. He leaned against the window and peered inside, pressing his nose against the glass.

"It's empty. The Fowlers will be upstairs getting ready for bed." Elijah looked through the window, wondering if a light had been left on, but the store was dark inside. Everything was in its place as he expected.

Mason groaned, then staggered backwards.

Elijah grabbed him before he hit the concrete.

"I can't lose him. I've left it too late. Too late." Mason stared up at Elijah, gaze unfocused, tears rolling down his cheeks.

"Mason?"

What the hell?

Elijah frantically looked around the quiet street. Should he call for help? Mason closed his eyes, his breathing slowing and evening out. "I'll call—"

"No!" Mason caught Elijah's arm in a vice-like grip. "I'm fine. It's just… you didn't see him?" He sighed. "Fuck, no. Of course, you didn't."

"See what?" Elijah frowned and glanced inside the shop again. "There's no one in there."

Mason struggled to his feet. "I'm sorry. Damn it, I thought… I'd hoped this would work out. I liked it here." He let go of Elijah's arm and stumbled down the street into the darkness.

CHAPTER THREE

Mason didn't think about the direction he ran, only that he needed to put distance between himself and Elijah. God, what must Elijah think of him?

The church on his left stood in darkness, the entrance to the park with its strong scent of camellias beckoning on his right across the road. He sprinted through the trellis, tripped on a curb and sprawled headfirst into a bed of soil.

Great. Mason sat up, spluttering dirt and flower petals. At least he was under a streetlight, so he could see enough to retrieve his beanie.

Not even twelve hours here, and he'd had two visions. That was a record, even for him. What was it with this town?

He hated his ability. What use was getting glimpses of the past? History was dead and gone, and nothing he could do would help someone who had already experienced it. He looked around, trying to get his bearings.

"Where am I?" he asked aloud.

Grass stretched for several metres ahead, the path and trellis behind him. Squinting, he made out another exit in the distance and the glow of the lights from the pub. Either he could go back the way he'd come or traipse over an expanse of lawn and whatever else he couldn't see in the dark.

One pat of his jeans pocket confirmed he'd left his phone at the B&B, so he couldn't use the torch app to find his way.

He stood and brushed wet grass off his jeans. The carved wooden seat under the street light looked similar to the one outside the Post Office. A copper plate drew his attention, and he bent to read the inscription.

Anthony Harwin. Forever Loved. Gone, but not forgotten.

"Tony was Kedgetown's librarian years ago," Elijah said.

Mason jumped. "Fuck, you scared me. I didn't know you were there."

"Sorry, guess I was stealthier than I realised. I came to check on you." Elijah gestured towards the seat. "Sit with me. You still look like shit. I was worried." He paused. "And to answer your question, you're in the park. Good thing you didn't go much further. It's dark out there. The only lights are the ones by the entrances."

"Yeah, I noticed that." Mason sighed and sat down next to him. "I'm sorry. I've made a complete idiot of myself twice in the few hours we've known each other."

"I don't think you're an idiot." Elijah rested his hand on Mason's knee, then looked down at what he'd done. "Shit, sorry. I do the touchy-feely thing without thinking."

"It's fine." Mason managed a smile. "I don't mind, honest."

He wished he had the guts to be himself and not hide who he was.

Like Elijah. He seemed a 'you get what you see' kind of guy.

"Do you want to talk about what happened?" Elijah frowned. "Or not. We can sit if that will help. I come here sometimes to think and enjoy the peaceful vibe." His face lit up when he smiled. "You should see this place in the spring.

The flower beds are awash in colour and have the most amazing scents. Perfect place to read, too." He grinned. "I'm sure Tony approves. Kind of apt, right?"

Mason chuckled. "Yeah, well, a librarian should approve of reading." A thought struck him. "I don't remember a library."

"It's part of the community centre in the council buildings. I'll take you to get a library card when it's open." Elijah ducked his head. "If you want one. Shit, listen to me. I'm planning stuff for you, and you haven't decided whether you're staying yet."

"I thought I might," Mason said cautiously. If he was, he needed to come clean. He couldn't settle in a town this size and have any hope of keeping his secret. Especially if no one else was in on it.

"Whatever just happened, I don't think any less of you." Elijah studied him for a long moment. "Anxiety attacks aren't something to be ashamed of. A lot of people get them, and if you're used to living alone… suddenly having people around can be a bit much. Especially someone like me who never knows when to stop talking."

"It's not you." Mason squeezed Elijah's hand. "Definitely not you." He chewed on his bottom lip. "I… this is going to sound crazy, especially as we've only known each other a few hours, but I already trust you."

"Whatever you want to say, you have my word; it won't go any further." Elijah glanced around and cocked his head to the side like he was listening. "We're alone." His voice softened. "A lot of people around here are used to keeping secrets. Whatever yours is, it's safe with me."

"Thank you." If Mason didn't mention the rest of his family, at least by name, he wasn't putting them in danger, right?

"I won't help you bury dead bodies, though." Elijah's mouth twitched. "I do have some scruples."

"Smartarse." Mason appreciated Elijah's obvious attempt to lighten the situation. "I…" He rushed out with the rest of the words before he could take them back. "I have this ability. I touch objects, and I get visions. I see their history. I got a weird flash from your aunt's spoon during dinner, and when I touched the glass at the bakery, I think… I saw a guy in there, and the shop didn't look like it does now."

"Psychometry? Cool." Elijah sounded excited and keen to know more. "I mean it. That's way cool. How long have you had your ability?"

"Since I was a teenager." Mason let out a long breath. "You're taking this very well. I didn't think you'd believe me."

"Why not?" Elijah frowned. "I've met psi before. But never someone who could read objects." He sobered. "You've never told anyone about what you can do? I'm so sorry you're going through those visions on your own. No wonder you wear gloves. Do you have any control over it?"

"None." Mason grew silent.

"Well, we'll have to do something about that." Elijah jutted out his jaw, a determined expression on his face.

"Umm, *we* will?" Mason wondered if he'd made a terrible mistake telling Elijah, but it was too late to take back the information. "And how? I've been trying for years and never managed it."

"Perhaps we could figure something out together?" Elijah shrugged. "I'm happy to talk through what you've already done and see if I can think of anything else. Sometimes another perspective can make a difference. You can't keep going through this shit by not knowing if touching an object will trigger a vision."

"I've tried turning it off." Mason wasn't proud of that

moment, but as he was being up front, he should probably go the whole hog.

Elijah raised an eyebrow. "Why am I not going to like this?"

"Because I was a bloody idiot, and I won't be doing it again." Mason looked away, not wanting to see Elijah's reaction. "I took some pills, a lot of pills. Luckily, a… friend… found me in time."

"Oh, *God*."

"So yeah, I figured once you found out what a fuckup I am, you might not want to help." Mason stood and began to walk away. So much for hoping he might have finally found a home and someone in town who understood.

"What the hell?" Elijah put his hand on Mason's shoulder from behind. "You are not a fuckup, and I'm going to do everything I can to make sure this ability of yours becomes something you can manage." He bent his head and whispered. "Sounds to me like you need a friend, and I'm offering to be one if you'll let me. Please."

A tear ran down Mason's cheek. "You barely know me."

"So? I'm in town for a few months, and you have a house to sort through, which I can also help you with. After that, you don't have to see me again, and you don't have to stay. But, in the meantime, it wouldn't hurt to have a friend while you're here. Right?" Elijah paused. "Also, do you need a hug? It's fine if you don't, but I figured I'd ask in case."

Mason nodded, choked up that Elijah cared enough to offer. Elijah slid his arms around Mason and held him tightly. He was a great hugger and warm as hell. Mason could do this. Having a friend would be nice. After he'd sorted the house and everything that came with it, he could go home and never see Elijah again.

"Right. And thank you."

~

Elijah felt bad for holding back his own truth after Mason bared his soul the night before. But telling a human, even a psi, about the supernatural community was strictly forbidden. If anyone found out, they would both be in a lot of trouble. The council was a pack of interfering arseholes, although Elijah liked Victor, the vampire councillor. The other two councillors, not so much if the alpha got wind of Elijah spilling the beans, he'd be called into Wellington to explain himself, pronto.

He'd asked his aunts once why psi had never been an official part of their community. While werewolves and vampires, for the most part, knew psi existed, they kept their own existence a secret. Psi powers differed between individuals, although some abilities repeated through generations, which made them an unknown quantity. Besides, there weren't enough of them to worry about. However, that hadn't stopped the human councillors keeping records of the ones they were aware of. As for working with them and giving one a seat on the council? Never going to happen. Imagine the chaos if a psi read a councillor's mind?

Elijah snorted. Psi weren't their enemies and had the potential to be powerful allies. At least Kedgetown had the right idea. Everyone held equal status for as long as anyone could remember.

He sighed and grabbed his jacket, ready to head out the door. Mason had already left for the house by the time Elijah came down for breakfast. Giving him a little time before barging into his space was probably a good idea. They'd both gone to bed early after getting home. Mason looked exhausted, and the day's travel had caught up with Elijah too.

"Elijah!" Annalise called to him from the kitchen.

She and Rilla both glanced up at him when he entered. He recognised the look on Rilla's face.

"No," he said firmly.

"But he could be." Rilla's eyes glinted with excitement.

"No matchmaking." Elijah sighed. "I'm not looking for a mate, and Mason's got a lot of shit to work through. And besides…."

"You'll know when it's the right time with the right person." Annalise handed him an insulated cooler backpack. "Lunch," she explained. "Sorting through the house will be exhausting work, and you'll need to take a break. There's a thermos of tea in the side pocket too."

"Thanks." Elijah opened and peered inside. His mouth watered at the scent of fresh scones and sandwiches made from homemade bread. "You went to the bakery this morning."

Annalise grinned. "You didn't really think I'd made them myself, did you?"

"Thank God, no." Elijah took a step back so he was out of reach of the tea towel slung over her shoulder. Aunty A was a great cook, but her baking left a lot to be desired. "I don't want to send Mason to Doc Scott's before he's settled in here properly."

"Cheeky." Annalise reached inside her apron pocket and handed him a large ornate key. "It's for the house."

"But surely Mason…."

"Sometimes one isn't enough. And you'd better get going, or poor Mason will be doing all that work himself."

Rilla looked like she was about to add something, so Elijah scarpered before she could. When she decided two people belonged together, being a ghost didn't slow her down in the slightest. Her psi ability worked a little too well with her desire to matchmake. But, she admitted, two souls being compatible didn't mean they should be together, and relationships needed work.

His breath hung in the air while he ambled along, enjoying the sun. Elijah wasn't a fan of the cold, but he could deal with it if there wasn't a driving wind behind it. He shifted the backpack on his shoulder and waved to Wendy, Scott's wife, when he passed the medical centre. Despite being away for years, he knew most of the people in town. They didn't get a lot of new arrivals, and the gossip mill would already be trying to work out Mason's story. Despite the townspeople all having overactive imaginations, they meant well.

The house taunted him with the smell of freshly brewed coffee and what smelt like breakfast bagels.

"Mason?"

Elijah got no response. Mason didn't answer the knock on the door either. Elijah peered through one of the windows, but the place looked deserted. He sniffed again, getting a whiff of the woodsy scent he already associated with Mason.

What if he'd found something which had set off one of his visions? He could need help.

Elijah pulled out the key Annalise had given him and turned it in the lock. The door opened easily, and Elijah stepped inside. Immediately, a welcoming blanket of warmth washed over him. He let out a sigh without thinking.

Home.

Dust cloths were piled by the corner, but Mason was nowhere to be seen. Elijah tilted his head to one side and listened. Music played softly in the distance, an older pop song he recognised. He followed the sound to a room at the back of the house and found himself at the bottom of a spiral staircase. A clear tenor sang along with the chorus.

Mason.

Elijah smiled, took off his backpack, and bounded up the stairs. A large open area about half the size of the house met him at the top. Mason wore Bluetooth headphones and moved in time with the music while he cleaned windows.

Sun streamed through the glass, catching Mason's blond hair and giving the illusion of a bright aura around him. He moved his head back and forth and sang about being home soon.

Wow, he's gorgeous.

Mason turned and froze, the spell broken. He yanked his headphones down to sit around his neck and turned off the music. "Umm, yeah. Hi." He frowned. "How did you get in? I meant to unlock the door for you, but I got busy and forgot. Sorry."

And cute with it, when he's embarrassed.

"Umm, yeah. Hi to you, too." Elijah forced his brain to work. "Aunty A gave me a key. I didn't get a response when I knocked, and I couldn't see you downstairs, so I came looking for you in case you'd had another vision and needed some help."

"Sorry, didn't mean to worry you. I didn't hear you knock." Mason indicated a couple of travel mugs on a nearby table. "I bought us some breakfast. This part of the house is set up like a separate flat. This is the living area. There's a kitchen through the door on the left and a bedroom to the right with an ensuite."

"Very cool," Elijah agreed. "You've been busy for the short time you've been here." He sniffed. "The coffee's still hot, too. Do you have another secret I don't know about?"

Mason chuckled. "I did about an hour's work, then went to the bakery to grab us some breakfast. Annalise said you wouldn't surface before nine. Looks like she was right."

"You're one of those… morning people?" Elijah didn't hide the horror in his voice. "We can't possibly be friends now. You wound me."

"Whatever." Mason grinned, and his cheek dimpled. "Guess if we're not friends, all that coffee is for me. I got chocolate bagels. Apparently, they're a thing. Who knew?"

"I *love* chocolate bagels. Thanks." Elijah picked up one of the mugs and inhaled. "The Lemon Tree hasn't lost its touch. Their coffee is still as good as I remember it. Aunty A sent food for lunch she bought from there too, so we won't starve."

"Weird name for a bakery." Mason took a sip of coffee. "Though I noticed they had a lot of lemon-based goods for sale."

"There's a tree at the back of the shop," Elijah explained. "The guy who bought the shop after the First World War planted it, changed the name, and it stuck. I think everyone just referred to it as The Bakery before then."

"Makes sense." Mason cradled his coffee close to his chest. "Using reusable travel cups for takeout is a brilliant idea. The disposable ones don't have the same vibe."

"We're a very small town. Mac Fowler has been known to hunt down customers who don't bring them back."

"Seriously?" Mason raised an eyebrow after Elijah nodded. "I thought he was joking. I'll be sure to return them then."

"Good plan." Elijah helped himself to one of the bagels. "If you don't mind me saying, you're looking much better today. Lighter."

"Talking to you helped. I haven't had anyone apart from family to talk to about my ability, and I…."

"Don't want to be a burden?" Elijah guessed.

"Yeah, something like that." Mason closed his eyes and took a deep breath. "There's something about this house, too.

It felt like home the first time I walked inside. It's… comfortable, for want of a better word. I feel safe here, and for once, I'm not worried about touching anything."

Elijah glanced at Mason's gloveless hands. He hadn't noticed the absence of Mason's protective layer until he'd mentioned it.

"I feel the same way," he admitted. "Not about touching anything, but about it feeling like home." Elijah remembered the key he'd returned to his pocket and fished it out. "As the house is yours, you'd better keep this."

"Annalise told me there were two keys," Mason said slowly, "but the wording she used was weird."

"Aunty A always chooses her words carefully." Elijah frowned. What the hell were the aunties up to?

"She said they were still waiting on the second key, but he'd be here soon, now I was."

"He?" Elijah shrugged. "You're right. That is weird, even for her. Who is the other person they're waiting for?"

"She gave *you* the key," Mason pointed out.

"Yeah, she did, but I'm not *the* key. This is." Elijah peered at the object in his hand and studied it. "Have you got yours handy? Let's see if there's any difference between them."

"Like key one and key two?"

"Smartarse." Elijah polished the bow of his key. "There's a couple of letters on here. I can barely make them out."

Mason retrieved his from his pocket and placed it on the table. Elijah laid his key next to Mason's.

"You got in using this?" Mason frowned. He pointed to the blade on one key and then the other.

"Yeah." Elijah looked at what had caught Mason's attention. "Hey, you're right. The blades are different, like they belong to different locks. They've both got the same engraving on the bow, though." He took them both over to the window to get a better look. "P, and I think the letter next to it is an S."

"PS?" Mason rested his hand on Elijah's shoulder, their heads together as they studied the anomaly in silence.

"Yeah. Like in postscript."

Mason met Elijah's gaze like he'd seen a ghost. "Hang on a minute. I found something before you came. It was tucked into a cranny in the bedroom. I only noticed it because of how the light caught it from the window."

He sprinted into the bedroom and came out holding an old journal bound in gold stitching. The title embossed on the cover was the same colour.

Something like electricity passed between them when their fingers brushed.

"What the hell?" Elijah looked up to see if Mason had experienced anything strange, but he was focused on the journal.

"It can't be a coincidence, and besides, I don't believe in those." Mason pointed to the front of the book he held and read its name aloud. "Postscript."

Mason carefully laid the journal on the table. When he and Elijah had both touched it, he could have sworn something weird had happened.

"You felt it too?" Elijah seemed curious rather than alarmed.

That was a good sign, right?

"Yeah," Mason confirmed after a few moments. Despite having told Elijah everything the night before and liking the guy, Mason couldn't shake the feeling Elijah wasn't being completely honest with him.

"Do you think it's the book or us?" Elijah picked up the

journal and examined it. "I can't see anything that might have caused that electrical feeling." He paused and met Mason's gaze straight on. "Like you sometimes get when you touch something metallic."

"Yeah," Mason repeated, his mind spinning into overdrive. He grabbed his coffee and drained the cup, waiting for the caffeine buzz. "No vision, though. Not like last night over dinner."

Elijah raised an eyebrow. "I thought the vision last night was connected to the spoon."

"Yeah, but…" Mason shrugged. "I thought it was, too, until now, but I've had this feeling twice. I don't believe in coincidences and especially not as I've had that vision before, too. It's the only one I've had connected to a person, not an object. I didn't get the electricity thing with the pizza guy, though, and I don't usually get it with objects."

"You think it's me and not the journal?" The colour drained from Elijah's face. "Fuck."

"What aren't you telling me?" Mason took a step back. Shit, he wanted to trust Elijah and had told him stuff he'd never shared with anyone else. Apart from Fiona and Nana.

"What did you see?" Elijah swallowed, his Adam's apple moving with the motion. "I thought… that spoon was Elard's. Considering how pale you were, I thought your vision might be from him."

"You're worried about what I would have picked up from an object owned by a *priest*?"

What the hell was he missing?

"Umm, yeah?" Elijah ran one finger over the embossed title of the journal. He opened it, flipped through the pages, and frowned. "Okay, weird. They're empty."

"You thought it might be a grimoire or something?"

"No! Of course not." Elijah looked up at him sharply. "There is a lot of weird shit in this world, though." His expression softened. "Did you see something that didn't make sense? And what pizza guy?"

"*Most* of my visions make sense. Objects have a history, and although I might not know the full story, I can usually put the puzzle pieces together with a bit of research. Like being shot, then finding out the person who made the object was killed in a robbery."

"Ouch." Elijah put down the book, walked over to the window and yanked the dust cloths off the built-in seat. "Come sit with me. We need to talk."

Mason collected the remaining bagels, figuring they might need a chocolate fix to go with the caffeine. He handed Elijah his coffee.

"Thanks." Elijah stared at the street outside before returning his attention to Mason. "We're two guys having coffee. The windows aren't open, so no one can hear us."

"That sounds suspiciously like you're about to tell me a secret I'm not supposed to know."

Elijah choked on his coffee. He glanced up at Mason, and his eyes glowed gold for a moment before returning to normal. "Shit. Sorry."

"That was *not* a trick of the light." Mason's first reaction was to turn tail and run. What the hell was Elijah? Definitely not a psi, but not a normal human, either.

The house ambience reached for him, sending calming tendrils, not only around him but Elijah too.

"I'm still me," Elijah whispered. "I'm sorry. I should have told you last night, but we're not supposed to." He held out his hand to Mason, who hesitated for a moment, then took it. "The house… this isn't an ordinary house, either."

"No shit, Sherlock." The words were out of Mason's mouth before he could stop them. "Sorry, I didn't mean to be rude. This whole thing has got me rattled. I… crazy thing is I still feel like I, and the house can trust you." He glanced at the floorboards. "Although part of me thinks I'm crazy for still sitting here. Should I be running?"

"You don't need to run," Elijah confirmed. "This house is old, and we're in Kedgetown. What I am isn't new to it."

"You're stalling."

"You haven't told me what you saw either?" Elijah squeezed Mason's hand. "I'd hazard a guess it's wolf related though, yeah?"

"A wolf howling and a full moon." Mason didn't pull away. He was more curious than anything. "Whatever you are, I'm guessing it's the same as the pizza delivery guy from a few months ago."

"Probably." Elijah still wasn't forthcoming with information.

"Elijah!" Mason had seen some weird shit since he'd come into his ability. "As I said, most of my visions make sense eventually." He'd suspected for some time that if there were psi in the world, there might be others who weren't quite human either. He took a deep breath. "You're not psi, like me. Otherwise, you would have told me last night."

Elijah looked up and met Mason's gaze directly. "I'm a werewolf," he mumbled.

"Seriously?" Relief washed over Mason. "I mean, that's way cool. I always suspected, but…."

His ability had reacted to contact with a werewolf on two occasions. Was it because they were connected to the paranormal world, too? Nana had said abilities occasionally responded in new ways, then settled again. Rather than being scared, he should embrace it and wait for the reason to reveal itself when the time was right.

"I thought I was the rambly one in this relation—*friendship*." Elijah flushed red. "Yeah, seriously. There are more things in heaven and earth than are dreamed of in your philosophy."

"Shakespeare." Mason rolled his eyes. "So, are all werewolves as geeky as you?"

Elijah snorted. "That's what you're taking out of this?" His shoulders relaxed. "Shit, though, you can't tell anyone I told you. I'd get in a fuck load of trouble if it got out."

"We've both got secrets, so I figure we're even." Mason frowned. "Is Kedgetown full of, you know…."

"There's a few of us, but we're not the only supernaturals in town," Elijah confirmed. "Other psi live here too, and some humans."

"No wonder I felt like I was home." Mason glanced around the house. "And what about this place?"

"No clue." Elijah shrugged. "As I said, it feels… it's more than a house, but I know as much about it as you do."

"I get the impression it's happy we've shared our secrets." Mason hoped his comment didn't sound too crazy. He chuckled. "Listen to us. Talking about this old place like it's sentient."

"You're a psi talking to a werewolf," Elijah pointed out.

"Point taken." Mason let go of Elijah's hand and retrieved the journal. "This is a clue, a big one. I'm sure of it. First, the keys, then this. It's too much of a coincidence to be one. If I believed in them, which I already said I don't." He brought it back to the window seat and opened it. "Hey, I thought you said the pages were empty."

Elijah leaned in closer. "Yeah, they are. What are—"

Words appeared on the first page of the book, written in cursive, that quickly grew into sentences and filled the page.

Mason glanced at Elijah.

"Read it," Elijah confirmed what Mason was thinking. "In case the words disappear again."

"Okay." Mason swallowed, suddenly nervous. "But if this summons something, you promise me you'll turn into a big scary werewolf and protect me?" He frowned. "You can—I did see a wolf, yeah? It's not an analogy for something else?"

"No. That part of your vision was right too." Elijah smiled softly. "I'll show you my wolf later. Promise."

He held the book open while Mason slowly began to read.

"Lewis Newman caught my attention the first time I saw him...."

CHAPTER FOUR

November 1938

Lewis Newman caught Cyrus Godfrey's attention the first time they'd met. Or rather, the first time Cyrus spied Lewis in his uniform, leaving the post office to deliver mail. Although Lewis had been in town a couple of weeks, Cyrus hadn't had a proper conversation with him.

He'd hoped they might when Lewis finally had mail to deliver to the bakery. Unfortunately, that disappointedly resulted in Lewis staring at Cyrus, blinking several times, dropping the letters on the bakery counter, and running out of the shop.

It had been a couple of decades since Cyrus had pursued anyone as a potential romantic interest. He tended to keep to himself since he'd fled Ireland after the Easter Rising and made a new start in Kedgetown. The town was refreshing in its acceptance of what he was, which was an added bonus.

Not only was he not the only vampire living there, but no one raised an eyebrow that the two men who ran the local grocery shop were obviously a couple. They weren't blatant about their relationship in public, but they didn't hide the sweet glances they exchanged either.

Cyrus watched them sometimes and wondered what it would be like to be in love with someone and vice versa. Nevertheless, despite how striking Lewis was with his blond, almost white hair and dark eyes, Cyrus would wait until he was certain his attraction was mutual.

He was a patient man. Or at least he kept telling himself that fiction. Something about Lewis had slipped through Cyrus's defences and refused to let go.

The bell over the bakery's front door tinkled. Cyrus glanced up, not wanting to be caught wool-gathering, and plastered on a smile.

"Morning, Rilla. You'll be wanting the usual, then?"

Rilla and her wife, Annalise, lived over Postscript when it was open. Cyrus had never seen them in the winter when the bookshop closed up and figured if they had a life outside the town, it was none of his business.

"Yes, please. One of your wonderful loaves." Rilla paused, thoughtful. "Lewis tells us you've been trying out new recipes again and that your lemon sponge is delicious."

"*Lewis* told you that?" Cyrus popped her order into two separate paper bags and placed them on the counter. "He's never bought anything from me."

Rilla grinned. "Ah, but he's keeping company with Anthony over at the library, and you know how that young man loves anything lemon flavoured. I do believe Lewis has been waxing poetic about your… recipes."

"My… recipes?" Cyrus hadn't missed the pause and doubted it was anything but deliberate. Rilla had quite the reputation in town as a matchmaker. He met her gaze and kept his tone even, ignoring his sinking stomach. Anthony and Lewis? But Anthony was courting a young lady from Greytown. Wasn't he?

Also, Lewis was human and new to town. He wouldn't step out with another man in plain view, even if he was inclined that way. Not when his world harshly punished such behaviour. Cyrus sighed, feeling foolish. If Lewis was interested in Anthony as a potential suitor, he'd be more likely to keep his distance rather than spend hours at the library.

Come to think of it, Lewis did tend to sit in the sun and read. A lot. So maybe he and Anthony were spending time discussing their favourite books.

A man could hope.

Although if Cyrus waited too long to make a move, he'd lose the opportunity to do so. Lewis had answered an advertisement for a temporary position at the post office. He'd only be staying a few months, probably less, once he discovered the true identities of most of the town's inhabitants.

"You've been the talk of the entire town with them." Rilla picked up her purchases and placed them in her basket. She didn't seem in a hurry to leave. "Some of the townsfolk wondered if changing the name of The Bakery to The Lemon Tree because you planted one in your back garden was a good idea."

"I happen to like lemons." Cyrus shouldn't need to explain himself, but Rilla had that effect on people. He'd heard rumours she was a psi, but nobody confirmed or denied it.

"And you've proven it's a good idea." Rilla glanced out the window.

Cyrus followed her gaze. Lewis had left the post office and was heading towards the bakery.

"It's been good for business." Cyrus swallowed.

Lewis's stride sped up. He looked like a man on a mission, with his head up and a determined expression.

"I'll take my leave, then." Rilla leaned in and lowered her voice. "Before I forget, Alan said to tell you he has your usual supply in his ice box."

"Thank you. I'll pick it up later today." Cyrus grabbed half a dozen lemon gems, threw them into a bag, and gave them to her. "Something extra for you and Annalise to enjoy with your afternoon tea."

"Thank you. I'll get out of your way then, will I?"

"That would be nice," Cyrus muttered under his breath. If he was going to make an idiot of himself in front of Lewis, he didn't want an audience.

She waved and passed Lewis as he entered the shop. "Ask him about his lemon curd," she murmured to Lewis on her way out.

Cyrus shook his head. Rilla meant well, but she'd always lacked subtlety. Lewis gave her a puzzled look, then continued towards the counter.

"Good afternoon, Mr Newman," Cyrus said, his mouth suddenly dry. Hunger accompanied his rising nervousness, and he wished he hadn't devoured his last bottle of blood the night before.

"Mr Godfrey." Lewis licked his lips, then chewed on his lower lip. He studied Cyrus for a moment. "Mrs Whitaker from the bookshop told me I should ask you about procuring a jar of your lemon curd."

"Yes, she mentioned it. Or rather Rilla—Mrs Beresford —did." Cyrus retrieved a jar of curd from the shelf behind the counter. The human world and its laws wouldn't accept two women being married to each other, or taking each other's surnames, but that hadn't stopped Rilla and Annalise from using Mrs instead of Miss. "Would you like something to go with it? Some bread, perhaps?"

"Bread sounds lovely." Lewis blushed, his cheeks a lovely sprinkling of pink. "I… I'm new to town. I was hoping you… er… someone… could show me around."

Cyrus raised an eyebrow. "Surely you've seen all of it

while you're delivering the mail." He mentally kicked himself. "I mean, of course, I'd love to."

"If you don't want to, that's fine too." Lewis frowned. He lowered his voice. "I like it here. The people don't seem very… judgemental about certain things." The earnestness in his voice and demeanour was sweet, although he was clearly embarrassed.

"You want to know if people here would report someone who might…." Cyrus chose his words carefully. "… not follow some of the conventions of society."

"Yes, that." Lewis glanced outside. "I, um, thought you might be interested in pursuing a friendship, but my apologies if I've misread the situation." He looked as though he was about to bolt.

"Kedgetown is a safe place," Cyrus said softly. "You can be yourself here, and no one will judge. The council are very choosy about who they allow to settle in town."

"I thought some of the questions they asked during my job interview were unusual." Lewis rolled his shoulders, his posture relaxing. He smiled, his face lighting up. "I'm sorry if we got off on the wrong foot. I've been rude, and I shouldn't have been."

"It's fine." Cyrus returned the smile. "It's a beautiful day out. I'll be closing the shop in another hour. If it's not too late, perhaps we could take a picnic to the park. I could make a thermos of tea for us to share." He'd always preferred to get to know someone before getting emotionally entangled. It made extracting himself from a situation so much easier.

"That sounds wonderful." Lewis hesitated. "Do you want me to bring anything?"

"Just yourself." Cyrus packaged up the bread and lemon curd into a bag. He shook his head when Lewis pulled out his wallet. "My treat for your supper tonight. A welcome to Kedgetown if you'd like."

"Thank you." Lewis gazed at Cyrus again as though struck by something.

"Do I have flour on my nose?"

Surely Lewis didn't realise what Cyrus was? His vision was normal, so his eyes weren't entirely black, and his fangs were definitely retracted.

"No, of course not. Sorry, I…." Lewis averted his eyes. "Never mind. I'll meet you outside the shop after you've closed then, shall I?"

The doorbell tinkled, signalling another customer entering the shop. "I'll see you then."

"I'm looking forward to it, Mr Godfrey."

"Cyrus. My name is Cyrus."

"Lewis," Lewis murmured and tilted his hat towards Scott, who was pretending to study the painting on the far wall of the shop. "Afternoon, Dr Kelly."

"Afternoon, Lewis." Scott waited until Lewis left, then grinned. "About time too."

Cyrus groaned. By the time he and Lewis set out on their picnic, the whole town would know about it.

Lewis straightened his woollen cap, took it off, examined it for specks of dirt, and then put it back on. He wiped his clammy hands on his trousers and took several deep breaths to slow his racing heart. Another check in the mirror confirmed nothing else was out of place, so he headed downstairs.

"Enjoy your picnic, Lewis." Faith, the middle-aged woman who owned the Fuchsia Boarding House, called out from the parlour as he passed by.

"Thank you." Lewis paused to give her a polite nod, then continued on his way out. Small towns seemed the same wherever they were. Back home, everyone knew his business or at least thought they did. He'd hoped he might keep a low profile in Kedgetown, despite the friendly greeting everyone had given him on his first day delivering mail.

He closed the front door behind him and took a deep breath, taking in the scent of the numerous fuchsia bushes in the front garden. The slight lemon scent reminded him of Cyrus, and Lewis smiled. The weird aura he'd seen around Cyrus must have been the lighting in the bakery. Meeting outside, he'd be able to get a better feel for who Cyrus was, or distract himself with other things and dismiss that part of himself altogether.

His hope of ignoring his ability had been quickly dashed when he'd arrived in town. Many of its residents had more than one aura, which was something he'd rarely come across before., At least a dozen people in Kedgetown were psi, given their purple aura. Rilla at the bookshop definitely was, yet Lewis had yet to figure out her ability. His parents had taught him it was rude to ask.

A few others had base auras that shifted between yellow and blue. Cyrus's was red like Alan's, the town butcher. Scott, the local doctor, didn't have one at all. Lewis had lain awake the first few nights, trying to figure out why.

Luckily, at least a quarter of the town residents presented the way he'd expected. Anthony was definitely human with no added extras, as was Gilbert, who ran the grocery store next to the bakery with Bevis, a psi. Gilbert and Bevis were a sweet couple, and no one seemed to mind they were sharing a house and, if Lewis's suspicions were correct, a bed, too. He wouldn't have dared give in to his own inclinations at home and risk arrest and prison.

Lewis sighed. He was tired of hiding so much of himself. His sister was aware he was a homosexual, but so far, he'd spared his parents any public shame. He snorted. In a perfect society, people would be free to love whomever they wished.

A sliver of hope trickled into the back of his mind. Perhaps he could be himself here in Kedgetown?

Spending time with Cyrus was the riskiest thing Lewis had done in such a long time. He'd had a lover at home, but they'd been careful to keep their relationship discrete. Then Terrance was offered a position in Auckland and moved away. In a moment of recklessness, Lewis considered following him, but Terrance wanted a new start, which didn't include Lewis.

He'd already walked the two blocks between King and Main Street before he realised he'd almost reached the bakery. Cyrus waited outside, holding a large picnic basket. He waved to Lewis and quickly closed the distance between them.

The wind caught Cyrus's hair, which he wore longer than the current fashion. He brushed it back off his face, adjusted his cap, and greeted Lewis with a broad smile.

"Hello. You made it." Cyrus greeted him, then shifted the weight of his basket into both hands. "I have tea, and I thought we could try my new shortbread recipe."

"I love shortbread." Lewis gestured towards the basket. "Would you like me to take that for you? It looks heavy."

"It's fine." Cyrus paused before continuing. "I'm stronger than I look."

"Do you have a favourite spot in the park for our picnic?" Lewis hadn't taken the time to explore much of the park, but he'd visited the nearby church a couple of times and briefly met the visiting priest, Father Elard. He'd struck Lewis as a friendly, gentle man, yet his aura was odd, like Cyrus's.

"Yes, although I'm not in the habit of taking a picnic there." Cyrus waved to Annalise, who was standing in the bookshop doorway chatting with Scott. "Our spending time together this afternoon will be the talk of the town for weeks to come."

"Is that all right?" Lewis didn't want to cause any trouble. "And I think it already is. My landlady told me to enjoy my picnic."

Cyrus snorted. "I'd swear at times that woman can read minds. Nothing gets past her."

"You think she can?" Lewis paled, remembering the thoughts of Cyrus that had filled his mind the last few nights. She didn't have an extra aura, so she couldn't be a psi. Could she? With everything Lewis had seen in Kedgetown so far, he was beginning to doubt his ability was working properly.

"She and Rilla have known each other for years," Cyrus said as though explaining everything. "They both grew up here, and nothing happens in this town that Rilla doesn't know about."

"I can believe it." Lewis heaved a sigh of relief.

Cyrus raised an eyebrow but, fortunately, didn't ask any awkward questions.

"The weather is very pleasant today, don't you think?" Lewis filled the silence between them more out of habit than anything. Walking with Cyrus felt comfortable, and Lewis had to remind himself they'd only recently met.

"If that's what you want to talk about." Cyrus started to cross the road, then took a sudden step back, dragging Lewis with him.

A couple of moments later, a riderless horse galloped through the street where they'd been standing.

"Need any help?" Cyrus called.

Lewis blinked. Alan Branton, the town butcher, stood by the horse, reins twisted around his hands. But he'd been nowhere in sight. How could he have caught the animal so quickly?

"No, it's fine. Thank you anyway." Alan patted the horse. "She's a bit restless today. A couple of the Fowler children have been playing around her stable again."

"Ah," Cyrus said. "One of *those* games, I take it?"

"Exactly." Alan grimaced. "You'd think old Daisy would be used to having we—the children there, but she's always been easily spooked. I'll have a chat with Fergal once I have her settled."

"You could always get Annalise to have a word with them," Cyrus suggested. "She's used to the little ones and their games." He grinned. "I seem to remember her encouraging the children she was supposed to be looking after and getting into trouble with her mam for it. Not that she was much older than some of them."

"Aye, that girl has always gone her own way." Alan chuckled. "Rilla's been a good influence on her."

"Love at first sight, those two," Cyrus agreed. "And a good match, too."

Alan, like Cyrus and Annalise, appeared to be in his mid-twenties. Yet, he and Cyrus spoke as though discussing something that happened years ago.

"How long have you all known each other?" Lewis asked.

Both Alan and Cyrus turned to look at him. Lewis fought the urge to hide from the intensity of their gaze.

"Lewis and I are on our way to the park for a picnic," Cyrus said a little too brightly. His usual red aura darkened as though whatever caused it was closer to the surface. "If you don't need any help, I'll leave you with Daisy then."

"Sorry to be interrupting your afternoon." Alan murmured something to Daisy in a reassuring tone, then led the horse back the way she'd come. A couple of feet down the road, he turned to Cyrus. "Don't forget to come by later for your package. Or you could join me for a drink if you'd like."

"I might need to do that. I'll call in later. Thank you."

Lewis waited a few minutes before curiosity got the better of him. "How long have you lived here? Your accent is Irish, yes?"

"I've lived here a long time, and yes, it is. Some change theirs, but it suits me to keep mine." Cyrus led Lewis to the park entrance. Roses bloomed on either side, a mix of pinks, lavender, and red. "Faith has put forward the idea of adding a trellis. What do you think?"

"I'm not much for gardening, but I guess it could work." Lewis stood aside for Cyrus to go first, as he obviously had a particular spot in mind for their picnic. "It's beautiful here." He helped Cyrus lay the plaid blanket on the grass a short distance into the park. "Has anyone thought of putting a seat here? Perhaps a long bench so friends could sit together and enjoy the sun on those winter days it doesn't rain." Lewis disliked having wet trousers after sitting on damp grass. It took him ages to feel warm again afterwards.

"Anthony's been talking about needing a seat since he arrived in town." Cyrus chuckled. "Everyone has ideas about what to do with the park to make it more welcoming. Most of them happen eventually."

"He hasn't been here that long, has he?" Lewis needed to defend Anthony for some reason.

"A year or so." Cyrus unpacked the picnic basket. The shortbread smelt delicious. Lewis took a piece when Cyrus offered the plate. "It's still warm, and you must tell me what you think as I adjusted the original recipe."

Lewis nodded, focusing on the buttery treat melting in his mouth. He swallowed before speaking. "Is it true you add lemon to everything you bake?"

"Of course not." Cyrus's eyes crinkled in amusement. "But I usually do at least two batches a day of something lemon. What's the point of planting a tree if you don't use it?"

"I haven't seen your tree," Lewis blurted out. He took a

large bite of shortbread and almost choked on it. Goodness, what must Cyrus think of him?

"It's behind the bakery." Cyrus unscrewed the thermos and poured them both some tea. He studied Lewis for a few moments. "Do I make you nervous?" He sounded more concerned than amused.

Lewis wasn't sure if Cyrus's reaction was a good thing or not.

"No... not really." Lewis wiped his hands on the edge of the blanket. Cyrus's aura didn't seem as noticeable in the sun, yet it was definitely still there. "I..." Lewis needed this job and hoped it might turn into something permanent. Mr Higham, the postmaster, had hinted it might if he and the town were a good fit. Could he allow his curiosity to put the potential of a new home at risk?

"Tell me about yourself." Cyrus took a sip of tea. "I must admit, you've piqued my interest since your arrival."

"Really?" Lewis raised an eyebrow. "You've... piqued mine too." Was Cyrus flirting with him?

Cyrus's cheeks pinked. The added colour was a lovely contrast to his dark hair and eyes and pale skin. "My apologies. I'm out of practice. It's been a while since I took afternoon tea with another gentleman." He poured them both some tea.

"I had a... friend at home," Lewis ventured, feeling brave. "Have you...." Goodness, he was so inexperienced at this. "Sorry. I'm not usually so direct."

"I find your directness refreshing." Cyrus took a sip of tea but didn't meet Lewis's gaze. "I had a... friend," he murmured. "He died a long time ago, which was one of the reasons I left Ireland." He tapped his thumb on the edge of his cup. "Life is so fleeting, and we waste so much of it. I'm not sure I want to continue doing that anymore."

"Is that why you asked me for tea?" Lewis had spent the

past few weeks trying to get up the nerve to speak to the dashing man opposite him, and now he had; it was like he'd taken his finger out of a dam.

Cyrus chuckled. "Perhaps. I'd convinced myself I was a patient man, and this conversation is thoroughly disproving it. But please, tell me about yourself."

"I'm from Denniston, on the West Coast. My father works in the mines." Lewis shrugged. "I did as well for a couple of years, but… it didn't work out." He'd seen the auras darken around the men with coal dust in their lungs, knew death would soon beckon, yet couldn't do anything about it. "I didn't deal well with being underground. Eventually, I left, managed to get a job as a labourer in Christchurch, and saved enough so I could finish my education."

"Are your family still there?"

"Yes, although my sister is trying to convince my parents to move somewhere more hospitable. Her beau lives in West-port, and the mine there is looking for workers." Lewis shrugged. "My father is a stubborn man, so we'll see."

"Hopefully, he will see reason." A shadow passed over Cyrus's face. "Stubbornness is not always a positive attribute."

"Your father was too?" Lewis guessed the reason for Cyrus's reaction.

"No, Da gave into the bottle too easily." Cyrus offered to top up Lewis's tea, but he shook his head. "My… friend, Donagh was a stubborn bastard though, when it suited him, and in the end, it was his undoing. He couldn't resist a fight and wouldn't back down from one." He smiled, though his eyes looked sad, almost haunted. "I was offered an opportunity I would have been foolish to decline. I looked for him, thinking I could share it with him. He was supposed to lay low and wait for me, but that wasn't who he was. You see, we'd committed to the cause, and by the time I found him, it had already taken him from me."

CHAPTER FIVE

"Vampires are real too?" Mason glanced up at Elijah, wondering what other surprises the journal held. When had Donagh died? The Irish had a long history of uprisings against the British.

"Yeah." Elijah flipped over to the next page of the journal. "This can't be right."

"What's wrong?" Mason followed Elijah's gaze. "Where's the rest of it?" He took the book from Elijah, flipped through the pages, then turned it upside down and shook it, hoping a clue might fall out. "Do…." He swallowed before continuing. "Is it possible there's no more because something happened to them?"

"I hope not." Elijah frowned. "The pages were blank before we started reading. Maybe there will be more later."

"There better be." Mason had finally found out something about Lewis, only for his story to stop almost as soon as it had begun. "The guy I saw in The Lemon Tree could have been Cyrus. He matched the description in the journal."

Elijah shrugged. "Maybe. He was crying that he'd lost someone, right? I'd like to think he lost Lewis after they had a long life together, but considering a war was coming… shit, we need to find out what happened to them." He grew silent, reached for the last bagel, and chewed thoughtfully.

"You feel it too, then?" Mason looked around the house. "I'm not merely curious about what happened to them. I need to know. And this place is connected. I know it is."

"Perhaps the aunties know," Elijah said slowly. "Neither of them mentioned they'd run the bookshop. They don't talk much about the time around the war either. No one in town does."

The journal had only added to Mason's pile of questions. He should have guessed the answers he sought wouldn't be easily found.

He blew out a breath. "You know way more about Kedgetown than I do. And I recognise a few more names in that book than I'm comfortable with."

"Why?" Elijah sounded surprised. "A lot of people have lived here for years." He paused. "Oh. You were thinking from a human perspective."

"I *am* human. Well, psi, but not a supernatural." Mason put the journal on the table, keeping a close watch on it from the corner of his eye. He took Elijah's hand in his. "Is that a problem? That we're from different worlds, I mean."

If it was, he needed to know now.

Before he got sucked any further into his growing feelings for Elijah.

"If someone had asked me a week ago, I would have said yes. Definitely, yes." Elijah didn't let go of Mason's hand. "This will sound crazy, but I feel a connection to you. When we first met, I had this overwhelming desire to protect you." He managed a choked laugh. "I don't believe in love at first sight and all that crap. Yet there's something…."

"I used to believe in soulmates," Mason admitted, "but after a while, I figured that stuff was for other people. Not me. No one, and I tell you no one, wants to deal with the shit I bring into a relationship."

"Try explaining to someone that you turn into a wolf every full moon and have to lock yourself up."

"Okay, that kind of puts it in perspective." Mason kept his voice even. "And anyone who has a problem with that, with you, is an idiot." He cleared his throat. "So, have you? Told any of your boyfriends about werewolves, I mean?"

"Shit, no. We're not meant to tell anyone what we are." Elijah looked panicked for a moment. Mason caressed Elijah's hand with his thumb. "So no, I never told anyone. I don't want the alpha on my arse, or worse still, the council." He hesitated. "There are cross-species relationships within the supernatural community. I know a few vampires who are married to humans. Werewolves and humans are rarer, but it still happens despite the pack being less tolerant than the council."

"I'm sorry. I know what it's like to have to hide a part of yourself." Something else niggled at the edge of Mason's thoughts. "How old are you?"

"Huh?"

"Annalise met Lewis when he first came to town in 1938, not later as I'd first thought. I'm presuming she's a werewolf like you?"

Elijah nodded.

"And the way you talked about Rilla in my room last night implied you knew her when she was alive, and she died forty years ago."

"I thought you hadn't noticed my slip." Elijah swore under his breath. "I'm usually more careful." He reached for another bagel.

"You already ate the last one," Mason reminded him. "If you don't want to tell me you're pushing eighty, that's fine."

Elijah looked indignant. Mason wondered what it would be like to kiss his scrunched-up nose.

"This is all new to me. Werewolves could live for several of my lifetimes." Mason let out a huge sigh to lighten the atmosphere.

"I'm fifty-two," Elijah said finally. "We age slower than humans but way faster than vampires." He stood and brushed imaginary crumbs from his jeans. "And fuck, what is it about me not keeping secrets around you?"

"This is my fault?" Mason rolled his eyes. Was Elijah serious or joking around? Sudden panic struck him. "Bloody hell. I'm sorry. I'm making you uncomfortable by asking all these questions about stuff that doesn't matter. I don't give a shit how old you are. I was curious, okay?"

"Okay. I haven't met a lot of psi either, so…." Elijah gestured to the journal. "We should probably clean up this place some more before we call it a day. I'm not sure whether we should put the journal back where we found it or take it with us. What do you think? It comes with the house, right? So it's yours."

"Ours." Mason had the oddest feeling the journal was trying to lead both of them to something… but what? He suspected it wasn't only to Lewis, either. "I'll put it back. Maybe that will encourage more of the story to appear. But in the meantime…." It wasn't the only source of information they had.

"No." Elijah shook his head.

"You don't know what I'm thinking." Mason frowned. "Do you?"

"No, but I can guess." Elijah's expression softened. "You want to ask the aunties, yeah?"

"Annalise at least, as Rilla…." Mason finally worked out what he'd been missing when Elijah spoke of his aunt Rilla. "You talk about her in the present tense all the time. She's not a werewolf though, or I would have seen her at the B&B. And you said she died."

"She did, but that doesn't mean she's moved on." Elijah made a noise between a chuckle and a cough. "Rilla's a ghost. Dying isn't going to stop her from doing what she loves. Not when she thinks there's a match she can make." He gave Mason a pointed look.

"A match?" Mason looked at him blankly, and then the answer hit him between the eyes. "Oh." So much for hiding his attraction. And Elijah had already admitted he felt something too.

"Exactly." Elijah packed up their morning tea and picked up the broom sitting in the corner. "And you want to encourage her by asking about Lewis and Cyrus, who were obviously on her radar too? I don't think so."

"I do." Mason picked up the journal and walked into the bedroom to return it to its hiding place. When he straightened, Elijah stood in the doorway. "Would it be so bad if she did? Try to get us together, I mean?"

"No, not at all." Elijah studied the floor before continuing. "Sorry. Lewis is family. You need to find out what happened to him. So, if the aunties know, we should ask them."

Elijah surveyed the room, contentment and the satisfaction of a job well done settling on him. They'd worked hard cleaning, sweeping, and dusting. The room shone, the furniture without its dustcovers, comfortable and inviting.

"It looks good," Mason agreed. The sun from the clean windows caught his hair, bathing him in light, as the warmth of the late afternoon sun crept through the house. "The more I see of this house, the more I want to stay."

"I was only going to stay in Kedgetown for a few months," Elijah admitted.

"You're not sure, now?" Mason tilted his head to one side and smiled.

Bloody hell, he was hot as when he smiled. Not that he wasn't anyway, but....

Elijah forced himself to focus and answer Mason's question. "I've never found anything worth leaving Christchurch for, yet there's nothing keeping me there either. My parents don't mind travelling. Mum's a Wayland anyway, so she's often up here visiting." He shrugged. "Aunty A has already said I have a home with them for as long as I need it."

"She told me the same thing." Mason shrugged. "Although I don't think it's going to take as much work as I thought before I can move in here. The photos didn't do it justice." He ran his hand over the window frame. "You don't get many houses built like this anymore. She's got way more character than the modern builds. I've always loved the idea of living in a small town in an older home, although my abilities soon put paid to that." His expression darkened. "I couldn't risk living somewhere where everyone knows everything about everyone."

"That's not something you need to worry about here." Elijah walked over to join Mason at the window. "There might be someone in town who can help you with your ability, too."

"One thing at a time, hmm?" Mason didn't sound convinced that was a good idea. "I've...." He took a deep breath in and out but kept looking at the street outside rather than at Elijah. "It's a curse, not a blessing."

"It doesn't have to be." Elijah reached for Mason's hand, warmth washing through him when Mason accepted the gesture. "I already offered to help, and I meant it. It's not a bad thing to be different."

"You have a community… a pack."

"You could too. Have a community, I mean. There are other psi in town here, and I bet there are more in the wider Wellington region. We could find out."

Mason squeezed Elijah's hand, then released it. He chewed on his lower lip. "I already know there are, but I'm not sure I'm ready to be a part of that yet. Fiona…." He turned to face Elijah. "My sister is psi. Most of my family are. I already knew Lewis was, but not what his ability was." Mason hesitated. "Fiona met Ennis shortly after she moved here. He sent his friend Noah a message when I didn't pick up my phone. Isaac, Noah's husband, is a nurse. He saved me from overdosing. They all did."

"Promise me you'll talk to me… talk to someone if you ever feel like that's an option again." Elijah shivered at the thought of Mason so desperate to be free of his ability that he'd take his own life to escape it. He chose his next words carefully. "Perhaps, when you're ready, we could contact them again. Together if you'd like."

Elijah had heard rumours of other psi outside Kedgetown, although they mainly kept to themselves. He doubted any of them were aware of the supernatural community.

"Maybe." Mason shrugged. "But for now, I want to focus on finding out about Lewis and getting this house sorted. Once I've done both of those and have a plan in place, I'll feel better about everything else." His expression softened. "I appreciate your offer. I'm not ready to go that far yet."

"Fair enough." Elijah leaned in and shoulder-bumped Mason. "Thanks for trusting me by telling me about your sister and her friends. I won't tell anyone, I promise."

"I know you won't." Mason sighed. "We're all keeping so many secrets."

"Both our communities have been for generations." Elijah

wished they didn't have to, but he doubted most humans would react well, knowing who lived alongside them.

"Yeah. One step at a time, I guess. At least we know about each other now." Mason peered out the window. "What time did Annalise say dinner would be ready? I'd like to talk to her before we eat."

"We'd better get a move on, then." Elijah glanced towards the bedroom. "Do you think we should tell her about the journal?"

"Let's see if she knows about it first, hmm?" Mason grabbed his jacket and retrieved his key. "Though given she gave us both keys, I suspect she already does." He frowned. "Cyrus said the bookshop was called Postscript and that your aunts lived above it. What if the journal isn't about the house but the bookshop?"

"Or both? The space downstairs would be perfect for a shop." Elijah frowned. "I've been there, in the downstairs part, I mean, before. I know I have. But every time I try to access those memories, they're out of reach or vague."

"The perfect space for a bookshop." Mason reminded him of the conversation they'd had earlier. "A bookshop called Postscript."

A delicious smell filled the air when they reached the B&B. Although Mason hadn't been in Kedgetown long, he already felt more settled than he had in years. He'd come home despite never having visited the town before. The constant feeling of being on edge was fading and smoothing over, to become something else. Something he couldn't quite put his finger on.

He grinned at Elijah as they hung their jackets on the hook by the door.

"How far away is dinner?" Elijah called out.

"It can simmer a bit longer."

Mason didn't recognise the voice of the woman who replied. He shot Elijah a worried glance. Their conversation could wait until Annalise's visitor had left, considering the mystery of the bookshop, and Lewis, was decades old, but that realisation didn't stop disappointment running through him.

"Get a grip," he murmured, then cleared his throat. "I guess we could make some tea while we're waiting," he said to Elijah.

A petite blonde woman popped her head around the corner. She was about their age and had a twinkle in her eye. Mason liked her already.

"Annalise already has the kettle on, and she bought some scones from the bakery."

"We don't want to impose if—"

Elijah followed Mason's gaze. "What the hell?" He turned to Mason, frowning. "I thought you couldn't see her!"

"Huh?" Mason matched Elijah's frown. "What are you on about? We've only just met."

"Rilla…." Elijah warned her.

"You're…." Mason glanced from Elijah to Rilla and back again. "But you're a ghost," he spluttered. "Right?"

Rilla giggled. "It's lovely to finally meet you properly, Mason. Come in, and have some tea. Annalise will be pleased by this development."

"Development?" Mason asked.

"Go with the flow," Elijah whispered. "It's easier that way."

"I can hear you, young man," Annalise called from the kitchen.

"Bloody werewolf hearing," Elijah muttered. "Sorry, Aunty." He followed Rilla into the kitchen, pausing in the doorway to gesture for Mason to join them.

Annalise was already pouring the tea. Elijah sat opposite her, and Mason settled into the chair next to him. He glanced at Elijah, who, after his initial reaction, seemed to be taking this expanding weirdness in his stride.

"Wonderful," Rilla murmured, helping herself to the remaining chair.

"How are you doing that?" Mason had always thought ghosts weren't corporeal enough to sit on furniture.

Elijah shook his head, then briefly squeezed Mason's hand under the table. Had Mason asked a silly question or overstepped?

"Sorry," he murmured.

"I really do like this one," Rilla said. "He'll do nicely."

"Stop right there," Elijah glared at her, but his expression was without heat. "If Mason and I decide anything, it will be because *we* decide it. Okay?"

"Of course." Rilla brushed her lips against Annalise's cheek. Annalise smiled, and her expression softened. They were sweet together, and clearly in love.

Would this be him and Elijah one day? Mason a ghost, and Elijah still alive because of his much longer lifespan.

"Don't overthink it," Annalise said softly. "You've had a lot thrown at you in a very short time, although you do have the advantage of having already dipped your toe into the supernatural world."

Mason gripped the edge of the table. "How did you—"

Elijah wouldn't have told them that Mason was a psi. He'd promised, and Mason trusted him to keep his word.

"You wouldn't be seeing me if you hadn't," Rilla pointed out. "Some humans who aren't psi, like us, can see ghosts, but that's rare."

"Not all psi can see ghosts," Mason corrected her. "And I couldn't see you before." He frowned. "I don't get why I can now."

"You found Postscript's journal," Annalise said. "And it revealed some of its contents to you."

"To both of us," Elijah confirmed. "We have a lot of questions, and both of you know more than you're letting on. What is Postscript, exactly? And don't tell me it's a bookshop. We've already guessed."

"She's a bookshop," Rilla said. "And a house." She smiled at Annalise. "We lived there once, a long time ago. I enjoyed our time together there. We did a lot of good, didn't we, my love?"

"Was Lewis a part of it, too?" Mason asked. "What happened to him and Cyrus?"

"Such nice young men," Rilla said. "And such a sad time for the town, too. First the war, and then the earthquakes."

"We can only confirm what you already know," Annalise added. "This is a journey you need to take yourselves, but we can give you a nudge and some guidance here and there, like giving you the keys. The rest is up to you."

"The rest of what?" Elijah crossed his arms over his chest. "And how did you find out Mason's a psi? You've said before that it's not always obvious." He turned to Mason. "I didn't tell them, honest."

Annalise took a long sip of tea before replying. "Mason's sister came to town last summer when the bookshop was open. The three of us had a long chat. Lovely girl. And as both Lewis and Fiona are psi, and given how you reacted to the serving spoon, Mason, dear, we figured you were too. Talents like that sometimes run in families." She frowned. "I hope you didn't pick up anything too scary from that spoon. Elard used it for a long time before he gave it to us. That boy has always had a sense of when it was time for things to find a new home."

Elijah snorted. "Don't call him that in front of him. He's way older than either of you."

"He doesn't mind," Rilla said, "unlike some of his kind who take offence at it."

"Vampire," Elijah added when Mason looked puzzled. "Like Cyrus." He cleared his throat. "So the house is Postscript, yeah?" He paused. "Although, at present, it's a house."

Annalise and Rilla glanced at each other.

"Yes," Annalise confirmed. "And you boys have the keys *and* the journal, which means she wants you to know her story, and possibly be a part of it."

"Because that's not creepy at all," Mason muttered. He went out on a limb. "Is that why I'm not getting reads from anything in the house but the journal?" Usually, with a house that old, he would have expected more glimpses into its past. "Not that I'm complaining…."

Elijah squeezed Mason's hand under the table. "You didn't think we'd find the journal?"

"We hoped, but Postscript either takes a liking to someone, or she doesn't." Rilla smiled. "Otherwise, she's only a house, or a bookshop, depending on the time of year. Not everyone is privileged enough to be a part of its magic."

"Magic…." Elijah didn't look happy. He moved closer to Mason. "You mean that literally, don't you?"

"Is there a problem with magic?" Mason figured if werewolves and vampires existed, why not magic too? "Isn't it a good thing?"

"I haven't had any experience with magic," Elijah said, "but the only time I've heard of it in our world hasn't been good. Mainly demons and stuff like that. The locals talk about Kedgetown having magic, but I've never seen it. I figured it was probably long gone, given…." He closed his mouth quickly, then glanced around furtively.

"Keep an open mind," Annalise said. "Promise me, you will. It's important."

Mason shivered when she met both their gazes with a determined expression.

"Okay." Elijah sounded reluctant.

Mason nodded, not wanting to express his agreement aloud. He'd read too much fantasy to know it might not be a great idea. Hopefully, Elijah hadn't made a huge mistake, but surely his aunts wouldn't put him in danger?

"You won't be going into anything without being fully informed." Rilla gave Mason a reassuring smile. "But you will have to forge your own path and decide what it is." She smiled. "For both of you."

CHAPTER SIX

"This is so frustrating!" Elijah closed the website window and rubbed his eyes. "There's next to nothing in the library archives about anyone who lived in the town at the same time as Lewis and Cyrus. And nothing much about them we don't already know."

"Do you want to grab some bread from the bakery to have with our soup and check the journal again?" Mason yawned and stretched. "I could do with another coffee, and they have the best in town."

"Sure." Elijah clenched and unclenched his hands. Shit, he hated this time of the month. He was always on edge the couple of days leading up to the full moon, and it had been ages since he'd shifted and gone for a decent run. Not that he shifted a lot, as he preferred to be in human form, but since spending more time with Mason, his wolf felt like an itch that badly needed to be scratched.

He'd enjoyed helping Mason work on the house over the past couple of weeks. Being around Mason was comfortable in a way Elijah had never experienced with anyone else. They'd talked a lot, and discovered books and music in common, but the silent moments between them didn't need filling either.

He gave a friendly wave to Wendy, the librarian, as they passed the issue desk. Elijah would be seeing her at the full moon dinner tomorrow night before all the werewolves in town took shelter in their safe rooms beneath the community centre. Scott passed them on his way into the building, a couple of paper bags in one hand.

"I can totally recommend Mac's lemon muffins," he said, pointing to one of the bags. "Wendy loves them." Scott grinned. "He's been tweaking some of the bakery's original recipes after I reassured him Cyrus would be fine with it."

"You knew—" Mason stopped mid-question after Elijah elbowed him.

"Enjoy your lunch," Elijah called, shuffling Mason out of the building.

Mason shot him a glare. "He knew them, and he was mentioned in the journal. We could have asked him." He lowered his voice. "Is he a werewolf or a vampire? As he's still alive and all that."

"If he was, he'd be able to hear you." Elijah sighed. Mason still had a lot to learn about Kedgetown. He waited until they were out on the street. "Scott's been here for as long as anyone remembers, but we don't ask. It's an unspoken rule. The older residents know about him, but they've earned that right. He and… others founded the town, but he's the only one left."

"Sorry." Mason ducked his head. "Fuck, I hope I didn't upset him then." He glanced back into the library. "Am I allowed to ask how he knows Wendy?"

Elijah shoulder-bumped him. "They're married. And it's fine. If he was upset, he'd let you know. Scott's a good guy, but he's straight up too, and doesn't take any nonsense." He grimaced. "I got into a few fights when I was a teenager. I was restless, and not great at controlling my temper. There was one boy at school who always got me riled up. Scott and Elard sat down with me and talked through some non-violent strategies for dealing with the situation. Neither of them sugar-coated the consequences if my behaviour didn't change. Kedgetown doesn't tolerate bullying."

"I hope the other guy got the same talk." Mason raised an eyebrow.

"Yes. He and his family left town a few months later." Elijah preferred not to think about that time in his life. He wasn't that kid anymore and had made an effort to change his path in life after Scott had shown him a possible future. "I modified my behaviour. He didn't."

"I'm sorry."

"I have an idea." Elijah plastered on a cheery expression. "Cyrus's friend, Alan, was the local butcher, right? We should ask at the dairy. That's where his shop used to be in the 30s. They might know something."

"Good idea." Mason brightened. "I'm surprised there was nothing in the newspapers about him, though." He frowned. "There weren't a lot of death notices either, and I would have expected a few stories about townspeople who had died in the war."

"Those often come with birth dates. We don't really do death notices for that reason, at least not in papers that humans can access. We have our own way of recording that kind of thing." Elijah wasn't enamoured by the idea of the registers each supernatural councillor held, although they did provide historical documents of werewolves and vampires in the region. He'd heard rumours there was a third register for psi and less common supernaturals, but no one had ever confirmed its existence.

"That makes sense." Mason peered in the bakery window,

then frowned. "The old photo on the wall is new. I'd like to take a look at it."

"Sure." Elijah followed him inside. Mason was right. That photo definitely hadn't been there before. He walked over to it, then glanced between it and Mason. The guy in the faded sepia photograph looked a lot like Mason. A closer look showed a few differences between them, but the resemblance was still difficult to ignore.

"I found it in a box in the backroom when I was looking through old recipe books," Mac Fowler confirmed. "He looks a lot like your friend, Mason, here."

"It's great-great-uncle Lewis." Mason studied the photo. Lewis was smiling, his posture relaxed. He looked happy. "Perhaps he did find happiness with Cyrus, after all."

"I hope so." Elijah paid Mac, then walked over to stand next to Mason while Mac made their coffee. "I wonder if they stayed here or moved away somewhere together."

"That's what I need to find out." Mason sucked in a breath, then ran his finger around the edge of the photo before Elijah could stop him.

Immediately, his body stiffened, and he started to shake. His eyes slid closed, and he collapsed. Elijah caught him before he hit the floor.

"Mason!" Elijah cradled Mason, stroking his brow. "Fuck." Elijah's fingers were covered in a fine sheen of perspiration. "You're okay. You're here." Elijah's voice wobbled. "You're with me."

"Should I call Scott?" Mac sounded worried.

"I…." Elijah hesitated. This had to be a vision, right? Mason wouldn't appreciate someone else finding out his secret. To hell with it. They'd worry about that later. "Yeah, and quickly. He's over at the library."

Mason groaned. His eyes fluttered open, then closed

again. He curled into Elijah's arms, his breathing fast and shallow. Elijah held him tightly, his heart thumping.

"Come back to me," he urged. "I don't know what to do." He glared up at Lewis's painting. It had to be the trigger.

Luckily, the bakery was empty because they'd taken a later lunch, although a crowd was gathering outside.

Mason opened his eyes again, his gaze settling on Elijah. His breathing evened out. "Hey," he whispered hoarsely. "You called me. I heard you." He struggled to sit up. Elijah helped him lean back against the counter.

"Bad vision?" Elijah bit his lip. Panic rushed through him. "Or is there something else you're not telling me?"

"Definitely a vision." Mason winced and rubbed at his eyes. He looked up at the sound of Mac's key in the lock. His eyes widened when he saw Scott, and he glanced at Elijah. "I'm fine." Mason struggled to his feet but didn't quite make it.

Elijah caught him as he swayed, steadied him, and lowered them both to the floor. "I asked Mac to call Scott. I was worried."

"A very sensible decision." Scott gave them both a kind smile. "Mac's moving the crowd along. Good thing he had the foresight to lock the door behind him after he let me in. The townsfolk mean well, but you don't need a lot of people around right now."

"But what if…." Mason trailed off. "Oh, yeah, right."

Elijah managed a grin. "That door wouldn't stop anyone determined to get in. Most of us are much stronger than we look."

"And there's a back door." Scott crouched on the floor next to Mason. "I figured, as you're related to Lewis, we'd meet properly at some point." His tone was casual, although he watched Mason like a hawk. "Your heart is calming, although it's going to take a while for your headache to go. I can give you something to help it on its way if you'd like."

Mason frowned. "How did you…." He glanced at Elijah. "Most doctors I know have to take vitals to figure out that stuff."

"I'm not like most doctors you know." Scott turned to Elijah. "He'll be fine, but watch him for a few hours. I'd recommend having your lunch at the house as another vision immediately on the tail of this one wouldn't be a great idea." He stood. "The two of you should talk about what he saw, too."

"I don't want any meds," Mason said. "I just need a few minutes to rest, like you said." His expression darkened, and he lapsed into silence.

"You're amongst friends," Scott reassured him softly. "Like Lewis and Cyrus, you're both important to this town. We take care of our own and keep our secrets. You have nothing to fear here, Mason. Isn't that right, Elijah?"

The question took Elijah by surprise.

"Yeah, that's right." Elijah helped Mason to his feet, not liking the way he was still shivering. "You're sure he'll be okay?" he asked Scott.

Scott nodded. "I've never lied to you, and I wouldn't about this." He smiled, and a sad expression flitted across his face, so briefly Elijah wondered if he imagined it. "Lewis is a good friend. He struggled with his ability, too. It will get better, I promise."

"I'll drop off your order at the house." Mac glanced at the photograph. "If you head there now, you'll have a clear passage. Scott's made sure of it."

"Thanks." Elijah glanced past Mac to include Scott in his comment, but he was already gone.

∾

Mason sipped his tea slowly. "I thought you ordered coffee."

"I did." Elijah shrugged, "but Mac sent tea. Guess he thought you needed it. If you like, I can grab coffee later when you're feeling better."

"The tea is fine, and I do feel better for it," Mason admitted. "Fuck, I've made such an idiot of myself. Probably in front of the whole town, too. Bloody stupid. I shouldn't have touched it, but… I was frustrated with our lack of progress and…." He leaned back on the sofa and closed his eyes for a moment, then opened them with a start when memories of what he'd seen replayed through his mind. "Shit."

Elijah edged closer. "That was a bad one, yeah? Next time, at least tell me *before* you take a chance like that, okay? We'll find another way to get the information we need." He bit his lip. "You scared me."

"Sorry." Mason ducked his head and focused on his tea.

"Does it help to talk about it? I can listen if you'd like. Or not."

"I've never talked about them before. Not since…." Mason smiled, remembering how Nana had listened to him patiently when he'd first started having visions. He took a couple of deep breaths to calm himself, the tea already settling him more than coffee would have. "I miss Nana. She got me more than anyone else ever did. I think… she got glimpses of futures, although she said because the future was in flux, those glimpses didn't always come true. She sent Fiona to Kedgetown, and said something about it being time."

"I thought she died a few years back." Elijah frowned. "You're sure she's not a ghost, right?" He looked nervous, which was weird for someone who was used to seeing them.

"Fiona's a medium, so I'm never sure. Some of the ghosts she talks to aren't hanging around after the afterlife like Rilla, but pop back for whatever reason before disappearing again."

Mason shrugged. "Although Gran mentioned something about a letter Nana had left for Lewis with another to Fiona about when to deliver it." He gripped his cup, his knuckles whitening. "When Nana gave me the hat you liked, she told me I should wear it when I visited Kedgetown. I never intended to come here."

"Your nana was a wise lady. I get the impression she and Rilla would get on well."

Mason laughed. "Oh, totally." He fidgeted with the end of the throw Elijah's aunts had given them for the sofa. He couldn't keep bottling up this shit, and Elijah had offered to listen. "This vision was a bad one."

"Something to do with Lewis?" Elijah prompted.

"Yeah." Mason drained his tea. "I was... surrounded by men in uniform. Soldiers. I could see colours around them, black, grey, like I'd stepped into an old photograph where the background had been colourised but not the people." His hand shook. Elijah retrieved Mason's mug and placed it on the edge of the sofa. "There was an explosion. A land mine, I guess. Blood everywhere. And...." His voice faltered. "I saw men dying, screaming. The same men I'd seen before greyed out. Lewis... he knew those men would die, and he couldn't stop it."

"Bloody hell." Elijah leaned close, then hesitated, and got up to pace instead. "The poor guy. Bad enough being in the middle of all that without knowing beforehand that those men were going to die." His eyes glowed gold, and fur sprouted on the back of his hands. He stilled, hissed a long breath, and his appearance returned to normal. "What you described sounds a lot like he could see auras. A psi with that ability in the middle of a battlefield.... Fuck. That's rough."

"Yeah." Mason shivered. He pulled the throw around himself, trying to get warm. "It did a number on me seeing it second hand, and only once. Depending on how long he served, he would have had years of knowing what would happen to the people around him." He met Elijah's gaze. "If he survived, he would have needed a lot of help to put his experiences behind him. I'm not sure you ever totally move past something like that."

"I'm sure you don't." Elijah growled low in his throat.

"You okay?" Mason hadn't seen Elijah on edge like this before. "Sorry, maybe I shouldn't have told you. Bad enough I had to see it without inflicting it on you, too."

"It's fine." Elijah shook himself. "This isn't you. It's me. I'm on edge because of the full moon tomorrow night. Normally I'm fine, but this month it's affecting me more than usual." He shrugged. "I haven't shifted for a while either. Been shoving the itch to one side."

"You have to shift on a full moon?" Mason searched his memory. "But it's up to you otherwise?"

"Yeah." Elijah grabbed one of the lemon muffins and downed it like he hadn't eaten in days. "I... we've talked about me being a werewolf, but...."

"There's a difference between talking about it, and seeing it," Mason guessed. "You've seen me at my less-than-brilliant best after a psi incident. You turn into a wolf. So what?"

"And on the full moon, I have no control over it." Elijah twitched. "Don't get me wrong. I love being a werewolf, but on that night, I don't. Once I shift, I have no control and no memory of whatever the hell I've done while I was a wolf. I'm a wild animal and a dangerous one at that, which is why we lock ourselves up. I'd kill you and enjoy it."

"Only on a full moon," Mason reminded him. He swallowed. "I need to avoid you on the full moon. Got it."

"Do you?" Elijah took several deep breaths. "Sorry, I'm being an arse." He shrugged. "If... this is what being with me is about. I've had a few relationships but walked away before any of them got serious. Can you imagine moving in with someone and then having to disappear every month without telling them why? And… umm… I don't want to have to explain my behaviour during sex either."

"Oh?" Mason raised an eyebrow. His mind went into overdrive. "You, umm, lose control of your wolf?"

"No. I…." Elijah looked embarrassed. "My last boyfriend thought I was weird and holding back when we slept together. He had no fucking idea." His cheeks reddened. "I… howl."

"Like a wolf?" Mason stopped himself from laughing in time. "Sorry, stupid question, and that's kind of cute."

"It. Is. Not. Cute." Elijah scowled. "And yeah, that's it exactly."

"Can I see your wolf?" Mason backtracked quickly. "If I'm not allowed to, it's fine, but… it's not just curiosity, I swear. I want to see that side of you." His heart sped up at the thought. "I… the more time we spend together, the more I want to know everything about you."

Elijah relaxed, a slow smile creasing his lips. "Really?" He sounded surprised.

"Yes, really." Mason stood and walked over to Elijah. He rested his forehead against Elijah's. "I know we've only known each other a few weeks, but… I think about you even when we're not together." He'd jacked off a couple of nights, too.

"Yeah, me too." Elijah brushed one finger down Mason's cheek. "You know more about me than I've ever told anyone before. Anyone human that is."

Mason leaned into Elijah's touch, his skin hot against Mason's face. "I'm not only human either. I'm psi. Between us, we have a shitload of secrets. You get what it's like to hide a part of yourself. I don't want you to have to do that with me."

"Okay." Elijah took a step back. He yanked his t-shirt over his head. "I like that shirt. This works better without clothes."

"Oh." Mason swallowed. "You're okay with me seeing you…." His cock hardened as Elijah toed off his socks and yanked down his jeans. "Wow."

Elijah's clothes hid more than Mason had imagined. He was well-built with muscled thighs and arms, and his chest was covered in dark auburn hair that disappeared into the top of his form-fitting black cotton boxers.

"Werewolves aren't worried about nudity. Humans are the ones with hang-ups about it." Elijah grinned. "And vampires get a bit pissy about anyone else seeing more than they should of someone they're with, too." He did a slow turn, wiggled his arse, pulled off his boxers, then straightened and faced Mason again.

"Fuck. You're gorgeous."

Elijah's eyes glowed gold. His appearance blurred. Mason blinked, and the next moment a huge grey wolf stood in front of him.

"Wow." Mason had sworn to himself he wouldn't step back or show fear once Elijah changed forms, but his reaction was unexpected. He grinned and held out his hand. How much could Elijah understand while he was a wolf?

Elijah padded over to him, wagged his tail, and poked his nose against Mason's shoulder. Mason dropped into a crouch and ran his hand through Elijah's thick fur. Now they were closer, the auburn highlights were more obvious.

"Your fur has a hint of your hair colour. That's way cool." Mason patted Elijah, then wondered if that was the proper etiquette. After all, Elijah looked like a wolf, but he wasn't one. He was a werewolf.

Elijah lifted his head. Their eyes met. Any doubt this wasn't Elijah vanished. Mason could see the same light in the wolf's gaze that he'd come to associate with the man.

Mason stood, an idea forming. Elijah had said he was restless leading up to the full moon. "When I need to let off steam, I go for a run. Would you like to do that? Together? Or do we have to wait until dark? Someone might see you and…." He trailed off, suddenly sheepish. "Oh, yeah, right. You're not the only shifter in town."

But not everyone knew, right? There were psi here and a few humans too.

Elijah shook his head. He gave Mason a familiar look and growled low in his throat.

"We could sneak out the back and keep to the shadows. There's plenty of bush around the park where we wouldn't be seen." Mason hadn't run for weeks. Perhaps it was what they both needed. He stood and headed for the door.

Elijah ran to sit in front of it, blocking Mason's way.

"What? I thought this was a great idea." Mason bit his lip. Shit, what now?

Elijah shook himself. A minute later he'd shifted form to stand before Mason, his expression less than impressed. "You," he ground out, "scared me half to death not even half an hour ago. And now you want to go for a run? Seriously, what is wrong with you?"

"I'm fine." Mason focused on Elijah's gaze or tried to. He licked his lips, swallowed, and looked Elijah up and down. "You're distracting me," he murmured.

"Do you want me to put some clothes on?" Elijah took a step closer. A slow flush spread across his body. Mason wasn't the only one interested if Elijah's reaction was anything to go by. "I should. Sorry."

Mason stepped to one side to let Elijah pass. "I meant what I said earlier. You're seriously hot."

"I…." Elijah hesitated. "I wasn't sure you were interested. I like you too."

"Oh." Mason blushed. He caught Elijah's arm. "Can I kiss you?"

"If we do this while I'm like this, we won't be only kissing."

"Is that a problem?" Mason let go of Elijah's arm. "I'm sorry. I'm usually not... I don't usually fall for someone this quickly."

Elijah grabbed his clothes and pulled on his jeans. Mason turned away to give him some privacy, although it seemed pointless, given he'd already seen Elijah naked. Shit, what was polite and what wasn't? He'd need to do a serious rethink, and ask a lot of questions.

Once he'd dressed, Elijah cleared his throat. "You can turn around now. And thank you."

"I don't want to overstep, or give you the wrong idea." Mason sucked at this. Secret keeping aside, he wasn't great at relationships.

"You're not." Elijah brushed his lips against Mason, then cupped his head and pulled him closer to deepen the kiss. Then, to Mason's disappointment, Elijah broke it and rested his forehead against Mason's. "That was a yes, to the kissing, I mean. I want you too, but I think we should take this slowly. We're from different worlds. I'd like to do the dating thing and see if this will work first. Is that okay?"

"That's more than okay." Mason leaned against Elijah, exhaustion catching up with him. "I'd still like that run some-time, if you want to."

"I'd love to." Elijah put his arm around Mason, taking his weight. "But you need some recovery time, and I need to get past the full moon. Then totally, yes, and I know the perfect place."

CHAPTER SEVEN

Another rumble of thunder rocked the B&B when Mason got up to stoke the fire. He settled back on the sofa, pulling the crocheted blanket around him. A wolf howled in the distance, then was quickly joined by more.

He shivered, took another sip of tea, and picked up his book, although he couldn't remember anything he'd read in the last hour.

"The first full moon is the hardest." Rilla materialised on the sofa opposite his. She met his gaze and smiled. "I remember when I found out my Annalise was a werewolf. I had no clue about the supernatural community back then. It was all rather a shock at the time, but I soon realised I'd been given a gift."

"I wouldn't think many humans know werewolves are real." Mason was glad for her company. He'd been going crazy sitting alone in his room, so he decided to settle in the living room instead. Elijah stressed Mason shouldn't go outside. Most werewolves locked themselves up, but he shouldn't risk it in case one had ignored the treaty. The B&B

was warded against werewolves on a full moon in case they caught a human scent and attempted to force their way inside.

"When I came to Kedgetown, it was the first time I'd left home." Rilla smiled. "Back then, life was a little more sheltered than it is now. In some ways, anyway. In others, I think we became aware of life's hardships sooner." She linked her fingers and placed her hands in her lap. "My father died in the trenches in Europe, my older brother at Gallipoli. It feels such a long time ago now."

"I'm sorry." Mason hadn't spoken to Rilla on her own before. He didn't know much about her. "I lost my nana a few years ago. I still miss her terribly."

"Lewis regretted not being able to see her again." Rilla studied the flames. "Unfortunately, second chances come with stipulations and a price." She glanced up at him. "Not that I'd change my mind about taking what I was offered. We did so much good and were given an opportunity only bestowed to a few."

"I wish I'd been able to meet Lewis. Nana talked about him a lot and their time growing up together. He sounded… lonely." Mason risked a question. "Were he and Cyrus happy together?"

Rilla grinned. "Nice try, dear, but I'm sorry I can't tell you that." She lowered her voice. "You'll find out in time. Have you read any more of the journal?"

"The pages are still blank." Mason hoped time would fill them, but so far, no luck. "I brought it with me tonight. I should have probably left it in the house, but with everything going on, I wanted to keep a part of the house with me."

"Elijah will be fine. He's been doing this since he was a child."

Another roll of thunder sounded overhead. Mason got up

and peered out the window. The rain wasn't letting up any time soon, and the wind had picked up too. Did Elijah sleep at all during the full moon, or did his wolf pace the entire night?

"Have you ever been to one of their full moon dinners?" Mason liked the idea of all the werewolves meeting for social time beforehand but wasn't sure humans would be welcome. Not that his going was an option, considering he wasn't supposed to know.

Rilla raised an eyebrow. "Elijah did explain to you what happens on the full moon, yes?" She fixed him with a stern look. "You're not to go near a werewolf or that dinner on a full moon. What if one of them changed early?" She shuddered. "It would be total carnage. Not only would you die horribly, but the werewolves who killed you would have to live with what they'd done for the rest of their lives."

"Oh." Mason swallowed. "I… Elijah did tell me, but…."

"All this takes a lot to get used to and wrap your head around." Rilla's expression softened. "Not all of it is easy, or fun. Often, love finds us, and brings with it a world of possibilities we never dreamed of." She chuckled. "Quite literally, in this case."

"Should we be talking about this?" Mason didn't want Elijah to get into trouble.

"We don't worry about the usual rules here. And you're with Elijah, so of course, you're meant to know. Kedgetown doesn't tolerate any of that rubbish about werewolves and vampires not getting on." She kicked off her shoes and tucked her feet underneath her. The shoes immediately disappeared, which negated the normality of her action.

Did ghosts choose what age they appeared? She must have been elderly when she died. If Mason hadn't known better, he would have sworn she was one of his friends from his uni days. Her dress was reasonably modern too, rather than what she would have worn in her twenties.

"I hadn't realised other places had rules about that kind of thing," Mason admitted. "Elijah has mentioned Elard a few times, and Cyrus was a vampire, too." If the mythology about vampires was true, Lewis would have passed away while Cyrus didn't age. Their happy ending would have only lasted a few decades, leaving Cyrus alone again.

"*Is* a vampire," Rilla corrected absently. "I can't talk about Postscript, but I can answer a few questions about our community if you'd like." She gestured to the fire. "Come sit back down and keep warm. Peering out the window won't make the storm pass any faster, and the werewolves are safe tonight. Nothing gets in or out of those full moon rooms until morning."

"Are there still vampires living in town?" Mason had met a couple of people he'd thought were werewolves, but he wasn't sure about them either.

"Yes, but more werewolves and psi." Rilla started knitting. One minute her hands were empty, the next, she held needles, wool, and what looked like the beginning of a scarf. "A few ghosts. Most have moved on, but a few of us decided to stay. I couldn't leave my Annalise, and we're happy together." She smiled. "I've helped a few people find love over the years. Mac's wife comes from a pack up north. I knew they had the potential to be a couple the first time I saw them. Those two lovely vampire gentlemen who run the dairy and general store are well-matched too, although relatively new to town. I was very sad when Bevis and Gilbert passed away after a long, happy life together. I still miss them."

"Were they werewolves or vampires?"

"Psi and human. We have a small population of humans too. Most of them know about our wider community, but newcomers have to earn that trust. The same goes for psi. Like humans, all species have good and bad amongst them."

"That makes sense." Mason watched her needles move, but the garment didn't appear to grow. "What's the supernatural treaty? Elijah briefly mentioned it."

"It's a worldwide agreement between parts of our community and the humans who know we exist. It's supposed to keep everyone safe, but unfortunately, it comes with a council." Rilla grimaced. "I've met a couple of decent councillors, but many of them are arrogant and have their own agendas. I keep hoping the next round will be better, and I've heard a few whispers, but it's not time for that yet."

Mason raised an eyebrow. "Not time? Do they have elections, or do you....?" He lowered his voice. "Do you know a precog?"

"That would be telling." Rilla wound wool around her fingers. "Unfortunately, they're not elected. Most stay in the role until they die. Or do something unforgivable. The council is like the pack. You don't want to cross them."

"I'll remember that, and hope I don't need to." Mason took another sip of his tea, only to find it had gone cold. "Excuse me, I'm going to re-boil the kettle. Do you want anything?"

Rilla laughed. "Thank you, but no."

"Oh yeah, right." Mason's face heated. "I forgot. Sorry."

"No need." Rilla laughed. "I think you'll be a perfect match for our Elijah. You're intelligent, caring, and accepting. Exactly what he needs."

"We're not together yet." Mason didn't want to encourage her, but the thought she might be right made him feel warm inside.

"You want to be."

"Yeah. I like him." Mason hesitated. "But that doesn't mean it's a given, okay?"

"Of course not." Rilla shook her head, amused.

Mason escaped into the kitchen. This evening was growing more surreal by the minute. His not quite yet, but wow they were dating, boyfriend, was a werewolf. And he was spending the evening chatting with a ghost. He poured his cold tea down the sink, then hit the switch on the kettle, emptied the teapot, and refilled it with another round of Earl Grey.

He leaned against the kitchen counter and let his mind wander. Would this supernatural council be pissed that a werewolf had taken up with a psi, even though it had happened before? Perhaps they were more tolerant of psi than humans without extra abilities, or were cross- species romances more common than he thought? Cyrus and Lewis were vampire and psi. How did that work, exactly? How many of the myths about vampires were true?

His phone buzzed, and he pulled it from his pocket.

"Hey, Fi, how's it going?" Mason hadn't talked to his sister since he'd come to Kedgetown, although they'd kept in contact via text.

"Hey, Mason, enjoying the weather?" Fiona sounded tired, although a hint of her usual bubbly personality still shone through.

"Yeah, holed up in front of the fire." Mason walked over to the fridge and helped himself to milk. "You?"

"I'm in Wellington this week. Business trip, so I'm staying with Ennis." Fiona yawned. "Long week. Ennis thinks he's found another few… friends, so we're keeping an eye on them."

They'd decided years ago to speak in code on the phone. Better to be cautious than reveal their secret. Fiona and Ennis kept an eye out for other psi but hadn't found anyone new for a while. Most psi they met had been drilled by their families to hide their abilities, which made them harder to find. Modern sensibilities had swapped out one kind of risk for another. Their abilities trod a fine line between helpful and dangerous, and many would be too easy to weaponise.

"That's good, right?"

"Yeah. No, that's fine. Thanks." Fiona paused. "Sorry, I was talking to Ennis. He says hi. You guys need to meet sometime."

"You could come to visit me here. I'm thinking about moving into the house soon. I need to get back to work, and it's nice and quiet. Plenty of space to set up an office." Mason wasn't sure what Ennis' ability was, only that he'd had some trouble controlling it at first. Unfortunately, all the psi Mason had met told a similar story. He shivered, remembering Noah's first teleport. He'd been damn lucky with that one.

"Maybe. Or I might come on my own once I'm back on your side of the hill."

"And?" Mason knew her well enough to know there was something she wanted to say and hadn't. Yet.

"Met anyone yet?" Fiona asked a little too brightly.

"Maybe." Mason countered her question the same way she'd replied to his.

"You have! I want all the details."

Mason refilled the tea and waited for it to brew. "His name is Elijah, and we're kind of dating. Since yesterday. Well, we will be. We haven't had our first date yet."

"Wonderful! You sound happier than you have in years, and I hoped that was why. So where are you going? For your first date?"

"We're going for a run." Mason hadn't checked out the one restaurant in town yet. Hell, he wasn't sure what Elijah's favourite foods were either. They still had a lot to learn about each other. "And I need to get back to Rilla. I don't want to be rude."

"You've met Rilla?" Fiona grew quiet, never a good sign. "She said you'd be able to see her if you were going to stay in Kedgetown."

"Do you know what's going on?" Mason frowned. "With Postscript, I mean. Did Nana put you up to all of this?"

"Nana told me you'd find what you needed there. I came to check out the town for myself and met Lewis. He told me that Postscript is a house or a bookshop, depending on the time of year. I figure there's magic involved or something, but whatever it is, the town feels right, like you'd be a good fit for each other." Fiona paused. "Let me know what happens, okay? If you need me, I'll be there. I'm not far away."

"Annalise said that about Postscript, too," Mason said slowly. "What was it when you were here?"

"A bookshop." Fiona hesitated. "If you get a chance for your happy ever after with Elijah, promise me you'll grab it. You deserve one of those after everything you've been through."

"Okay." Mason trusted her instincts, and her offer to help out wouldn't have been made lightly. "See you soon, though? Miss you. And I'd like you to meet Elijah sooner rather than later."

"Yeah. I'd like that too. Love you, and look after yourself. 'Bye." The phone went dead.

"'Bye." Mason shoved his phone back into his pocket. He poured more tea, cleared the kitchen while it brewed, and then headed back into the living room. "Sorry, that took a while. My sister rang."

"Fiona's a lovely girl." Rilla smiled. "I can see some of Lewis in both of you, although she doesn't have his colouring."

"Can I ask you something? I know you can't answer all of

my questions directly, but surely a yes or no can't hurt, right?"

"I suppose not." Rilla put down her knitting. "I'm sorry, but you do have to find your own way. It's the way the magic works."

"I get that, but I'm getting frustrated by it, too." Mason took a few moments to formulate his question. "Is Postscript the key to what happened to Lewis?"

"Yes." Rilla sighed. "I'm sorry. I wish I could tell you more, but I can't."

Okay then. That was progress.

"When did he die?" If Mason had a date, it might help to find him.

"No."

Mason frowned. "Excuse me? You mean you can't tell me, or… do I have to rephrase my question, so it's yes or no?"

"No." Rilla sighed. "You'll know everything in a few months. Be patient. It will be worth it. I remember getting very annoyed by the whole thing. I threw that bloody journal at the wall at one point too. Annalise and I had our first argument over it."

"I might go fetch the thing now to see if there's another chapter to read." Mason hesitated. "You don't mind, do you? Considering you have a history with the house, too. I don't want to bring up any bad memories for you."

If there was something new, he could read it now and then share it again with Elijah later. Mason glanced at his watch. Morning wasn't that far away. He wasn't sleepy and doubted he'd settle until Elijah got back anyway. Perhaps Lewis and Cyrus could tell him more than Rilla was allowed to.

"Of course not, and most of my memories of it are happy ones. I'm sure yours will be, too." Rilla bundled up her knitting. "If you want some privacy while you read, I can disappear and return if you need me."

"It's fine." He was enjoying her company. "I'll read, and you can knit, if that's okay with you."

"Perfect." Rilla beamed. "It's lovely to have company again on a full moon. Thank you."

CHAPTER EIGHT

March 1939

"You should tell him." Victor Rochford closed the bakery accounting ledger and joined Cyrus at the window to watch the backyard cricket game in the garden area outside. "He's a welcome addition to the town, and more importantly, you have a spring in your step again."

Lewis chatted with Victor's wife, Esmé, while they watched Adam Latimer's young daughter playing with one of the Fowler children. Adam and his wife, Harriet, had arrived in Kedgetown a few months ago with nowhere to go and no family to ask for support. Cyrus offered Adam a job as his apprentice in the bakery, and the town council found them permanent lodgings.

"I am enjoying being able to take a break occasionally, but Adam doesn't need to—"

Victor pinched the bridge of his nose. "Don't be dense, Cyrus." He and Cyrus had known each other for over twenty years. As well as Victor being Cyrus's accountant, they'd become good friends. "I know love when I see it, and Lewis is definitely in love with you." His voice softened. "And you with him."

Although Victor appeared to be in his late twenties, he was closer to a hundred and fifty, so a couple of decades younger than Cyrus. Their age difference didn't stop Victor giving advice when he thought Cyrus needed it.

"Maybe," Cyrus said cautiously.

Lewis laughed at something Esmé said, then reached up to catch the ball eleven-year-old Fergus Fowler batted in his direction. He ruffled the boy's head when Fergus ran over to collect the ball before handing it back. The children loved Lewis's gentle nature, and the way he'd often join in their games. He'd had a turn at batting during their latest round of cricket, then convinced Adam to take over. Audrey Latimer gripped the cricket bat now, her father guiding her movements from behind. The seven-year-old was determined to give anything a go. The way everyone worked together was endearing, although Cyrus quickly dismissed the memories of his own family. They were long gone, and he wanted to focus on the present, not the past.

"I told Esmé I'm a vampire not long after we started courting," Victor said. "She'd guessed there was something I wasn't telling her, and while I hadn't lied to her, I hadn't found the courage to tell her the truth either." He smiled. "She was more concerned about how marrying her would affect me as she would age while I didn't."

"You've never thought of turning her?" Cyrus had steered clear of romance since he'd lost Donagh during the Wexford Rebellion in 1798. He'd met up with a few men for sex in brothels and back alleys, but made sure never to be with the same person twice. Although he was well-practised at hiding his vampire and could use thrall to make his partner forget, he preferred not to risk incarceration. While the Supernatural Council had no problem with those in their community being homosexual, they took a dim view of anyone running foul of the human legal system. One of the reasons supernaturals had survived so long was because they'd kept their existence a secret.

"We've discussed it, but decided against it." Victor smiled. "We have plenty of time ahead of us to change our minds. But for now, we're content the way we are." He returned Esmé's wave. "It's not good to live a very long life alone."

"I'm not alone. I have friends who *usually* give me good advice."

Victor chuckled. "Even if you don't often listen." He tipped his head to one side, listening. "I believe we are about to be invaded."

"That's why I made a batch of scones earlier." Cyrus moved at vampire speed, retrieved the tea towel filled with baking, and laid it on the table. "You'd better get in quickly. Those children always have huge appetites."

"I've never met a werewolf who doesn't." Victor sensibly got out of the way as small feet pounded across the lawn towards the bakery. "Can I get you some tea, dear?" he asked his wife.

"We'd all like some, and I can help. If Cyrus doesn't mind me taking over, that is." Esmé stood back to let the children into the house.

"Of course not. Make yourself at home." Cyrus peered past her, looking for Lewis. "There's butter and lemon curd for the scones, too."

"You should go help him tidy up," Victor said in a low voice after he'd exchanged a look with Esmé. "Adam's helping Audrey in the parlour, so Lewis is all alone out there."

Cyrus sensed a conspiracy but had enough sense not to protest. At least out loud. "Of course, he is."

"Those children are full of energy." Lewis was on his hands and knees retrieving a ball from under a nearby bush. "They're also much stronger than I anticipated." He stood, ball in hand and dusted off his trousers. Cyrus retrieved Lewis's cap and handed it back to him. "It's very kind of you to look after the children while Mrs Fowler is busy with her babies. I still can't believe she's had triplets."

"We help each other out around here." Cyrus shrugged, not wanting to make more of it than what it was. "We always have." He brushed his lips against Lewis's cheek, smiling when Lewis blushed. He loved how responsive Lewis was to his touch.

Lewis glanced around, then took Cyrus's hand in his and brought it to his lips. "I like what we have together." He swallowed. "There's something I've been meaning to tell you, but it never seemed the right time. You've always been so busy with the bakery, and then this morning your friend Victor was already here by the time I'd finished my postal round."

"Is Victor being here a problem? He and Esmé will be heading back to Wellington in the morning." Cyrus had offered them his guest room like he always did when they visited.

"No, no. Of course not. I like them. They're very nice. Kind too." Lewis dropped the ball into the basket by the clothesline, then grew quiet.

"What did you want to talk to me about?" Cyrus prompted. With the windows open, any conversation they had would probably be overheard. "Do you want to go somewhere else?" He hesitated. "If it's something private, we should probably go somewhere else."

"No, I'm fine staying here, if you are." Lewis gave Cyrus a shy smile. "Staying in town is what I want to talk about, actually. I have a permanent job at the Post Office if I want to stay. I'd like to, but I wanted to talk to you first."

"Of course, I want you to stay." Cyrus frowned. "Why would you think I wouldn't?" Victor's advice echoed in Cyrus's mind, but he ignored it. For now.

"I can't stay at the boarding house indefinitely either."

"Move in with me," Cyrus said quickly. "Most of the town already knows we're courting, and… but only if you want to." He laid his hand over Lewis's heart. "I can set up the spare room if you don't—"

"If I'm moving in with you, I will not be your lodger." Lewis rolled his eyes. "Do you honestly think I could sleep with you across the hallway?" He kissed Cyrus soundly on the lips. "We've been stepping out for months now, and the more time I spend with you, the harder it is to not take our relationship further." He cleared his throat, his heart speeding up. "Although…."

Cyrus growled low in his throat. He and Lewis weren't soulmates, or they wouldn't have been able to take their relationship this slowly. Even so, the idea of Lewis leaving had given Cyrus several restless nights. He didn't want to imagine his life without Lewis. *Blast it!* Victor was right.

"I love you." Cyrus spoke the words for the first time, surprised by how easily they fell from his lips.

"I kind of figured…." Lewis blushed, his cheeks dusting a delightful pink. It made him look alluring, and yet vulnerable, too. "That's one of the reasons I want to stay in Kedgetown. I felt miserable at the thought of leaving you." He took a deep breath. "I love you too."

"You're very easy to love." Cyrus took Lewis's hand and squeezed it. "But we do need to talk before we make a decision. There's something I need to tell you."

"I haven't exactly been honest with you about everything either." Lewis ducked his head. "It's nothing… well it is, but… I still want to be with you, if you still want to."

"Wait until everyone's left, and we'll talk."

Lewis took a step back and studied Cyrus intently.

A lump caught in Cyrus's throat at the fierceness of Lewis's gaze.

"I'm not going anywhere, I promise." He kissed Lewis's brow.

"I know, but...." Lewis wrapped his arms around Cyrus and held him tightly. "Sorry, I'm being silly," he murmured after letting go. "Let's go help pack up inside, and get everyone on their way. "I don't suppose you have any of those scones to go?"

"Go?" Cyrus looked at him blankly. "You don't need to go." Victor was spending the evening out with Alan. "Stay for dinner. Please."

Lewis hesitated, then smiled. "I'd love to."

"Elard's invited us over to the presbytery for the evening." Victor said casually over dinner.

Elard only came to town every few months as he had his own parish to attend to in Napier. Lewis had only met him a few times. He had an interesting view of the world, and Lewis enjoyed the conversations they'd had.

"I didn't know he was in town." Cyrus raised an eyebrow. "I thought you were spending the evening with Alan."

Lewis hid his pleasure at the thought of an evening to themselves, then worried that Cyrus might miss out. "Do you want to go?"

"I'll see him tomorrow." Cyrus smiled and briefly squeezed Lewis's knee under the table.

"Elard arrived late this afternoon. Alan's going to come with us as it's a good opportunity for all of us to meet up.

Esmé and I don't get to Kedgetown as often as we'd like, so we're looking forward to it." Victor swallowed a mouthful of chicken pie. "This is delicious, as usual. Baked to perfection."

Esmé brushed her hand against Victor's right arm. "Enjoy your evening alone with Cyrus," she whispered to Lewis. They were a sweet couple, and very obviously in love. "It's totally a social call, despite recent events. I try to keep out of the other business, as it's a little too political at times for my liking."

"Most of us share that sentiment." Cyrus grimaced. "My apologies," he said to Lewis. "We have some mutual… friends… who are causing some trouble. I'll explain later."

"No problem." Lewis speared a green bean with his fork. Friendship usually came with a shared history. If Cyrus wasn't repelled by what Lewis was, hopefully, they'd have many years together to learn more about each other's pasts. Seeing Victor and Esmé together, and openly affectionate with each other made him realise how much he wanted that with Cyrus. "How long have you been friends? Cyrus's explanation of how you met is a little vague."

"It's rather amusing, actually." Victor looked sheepish. "We met in Dublin some time ago. I'd bought a berth on a ship to New Zealand and lost my ticket in a card game to Cyrus. For someone good with figures, I'm surprisingly bad at games of chance."

"That game is as much about skill as chance," Cyrus pointed out. "Anyway, imagine my surprise when I was looking for an accountant, and Victor answered my advertisement."

"He had the nerve to offer to play another hand of poker." Victor rolled his eyes. "Like I'd be foolish to set myself up to be robbed again?"

"Luck of the Irish," Cyrus sounded smug. He winked at Lewis. "Or so I've heard."

"They decided to put the past behind them and gained a friendship." Esmé chuckled. "Although they never agree about what really happened when they first met. I've heard all sorts of tall stories about that day."

"It wasn't my fault the game was cut short because Cyrus forgot to mention why he was in a hurry to leave the country."

"Or that you neglected to tell me you were working for the very men I was trying to avoid."

"I was planning to leave," Victor protested. "Hence the ticket I lost to you. We ended up leaving the establishment with more haste than we intended, with an upturned table, and on the run as both sides thought we were consorting with the enemy."

"The table was upended *during* the game?" Lewis hadn't missed the deliberate vagueness around the identity of their employers.

"Ah, yes. About that." Cyrus grinned. "While I would have clearly won, Victor didn't believe me, so we cut a deck. Highest card won."

"I laid low and booked passage on the next sailing. It was definitely time to move on." Victor didn't seem angry over what had happened. "Truth be told, he needed that ticket more than I did, so I let him have it."

Cyrus stared at him. "You've never told me that before. I thought…." He seemed honestly taken aback.

"My Victor is a good man," Esmé said softly. "He can never resist someone in need, no matter who they are."

"Not to mention how much I disliked what we were doing in Ireland. I'd been a soldier for too long, and needed a new start. Meeting Cyrus enforced the feeling that my desire to leave was the right one." Victor and Esmé shared a smile. "If I hadn't come to New Zealand, I wouldn't have met my Esmé, and now I have a good friend in Cyrus too."

"Friendships and family are important," Lewis agreed. He slipped his hand into his pocket, his fingers closing over the letter his sister, Louisa, had sent him that morning. "None of us knows how much time we have left," he ventured. "Or what might be ahead."

"That sentiment isn't like you." Cyrus frowned. "I hope what you're wanting to tell me isn't connected to bad news."

"I don't think so." Lewis didn't want to say too much in front of Cyrus's friends. He took another sip of wine. Esmé's aura was delicate pink, unlike her husband's, who wore the same red as Cyrus, although the shade was a little paler.

"Do you want us to take dessert to Elard's?" Esmé asked. "He always enjoys your creations, and you and Lewis would have more time together."

"You don't have to leave early on my account," Lewis said.

"Ah, yes, but once you decide to bare your soul to someone, it's best done without too much delay." Victor's mouth twitched, and he gave Cyrus a long look.

Esmé kicked her husband under the table. "He makes it sound like we're about to run away in the next few minutes, which we're not. Of course, we're staying to help with the dishes first. You cooked us a lovely meal. It's the least we can do."

"I can help Cyrus with the dishes," Lewis assured her. "You're his visitors, and you'd have more time with your friends this way."

Cyrus glanced between them. "I know when I'm outnumbered. And I know better than to argue with Esmé. She is quite the force to be reckoned with once she sets her mind on something. Or someone."

Victor smiled. "I noticed that the first time we met." He wiped his lips with his serviette and drained his wine. "Alan has procured a wonderful red for us to share tonight. I can get him to put aside a smaller bottle for you, Cyrus, if you'd like."

"Thank you. I appreciate that." Cyrus glanced at Lewis, then murmured so softly that Lewis almost missed it. "I suspect I might need it."

CHAPTER NINE

"I like your friends." Lewis poured himself and Cyrus some coffee. Once the dishes were finished, they'd retired to the living room with the remains of the sponge cake Cyrus had made for dessert. Lewis almost suggested they talk first, but he didn't want to leave Cyrus alone to deal with the aftermath of dinner *and* their conversation if everything went horribly wrong between them.

"They like you too." Cyrus gulped some coffee.

"Careful," Lewis warned too late. "That's hot."

"It's fine." Cyrus nursed the cup and shuffled to the other end of the sofa. Whatever he wanted to talk to Lewis about had him on edge.

"I'll go first, then, shall I?" Lewis hated seeing Cyrus so nervous. Getting one revelation out of the way might ease the tension.

"If you want to." Cyrus got up and switched on the light. "Better for you to see," he explained. "I didn't realise how dark it was."

His eyes looked unusual in the light, not quite right, as though his irises had expanded to take over the entire surface. Lewis blinked and looked again, but on second glance, they seemed normal. He was seeing things. More than he usually did, anyway.

Lewis hesitated. How could he tell Cyrus the truth without sounding like a complete idiot? Best to get it over and done with.

"I see auras." The words spilled out in a rush. Lewis took a breath and kept going. In for a penny, in for a pound, and all that. "Yours is red, and I don't know why. I'm guessing it's something to do with whatever it is you want to tell me." He swallowed, surprised at the relieved expression Cyrus wore. "Or not," Lewis trailed off awkwardly. He took a large mouthful of coffee and forced himself to meet Cyrus's eyes, which were definitely not looking normal by any stretch of the imagination.

"You're psi. That makes this a lot easier." Cyrus placed one hand on Lewis's knee. Cyrus's touch was cold, despite the room being warm.

Lewis had always dismissed Cyrus's cooler body temperature because he didn't want to think about what that might mean. He'd figured if Cyrus had some medical condition, he'd mention it in due course.

Goodness, his thoughts were rambling now, too. Lewis took a sip of coffee, and then Cyrus's words sunk in. "You know about us?" Lewis frowned, yet didn't feel the urge to run. Bloody hell, this was Cyrus. Lewis didn't have anything to fear from Cyrus. They were friends. And hopefully, more. "But how? We're not supposed to tell anyone. It's dangerous."

Cyrus silenced Lewis with a brief kiss. "The same way *we're* not supposed to tell anyone about us," he said softly.

"Us?" Lewis studied Cyrus. "I'm not imagining your eyes, am I? They're entirely black. No white at all."

"You're not scared?"

"No. I think it's rather… enticing… actually." Lewis licked

his lips and forced himself to focus on Cyrus's words, not his own rather obvious physical reaction to their proximity. "Does it hurt?"

Cyrus shook his head. He glanced at the floor. When he met Lewis's gaze again, Cyrus's teeth looked different, too.

"You have fangs." Lewis put down his coffee with a thump. "What did you add to this?"

"I haven't drugged you." Cyrus sounded amused. "You accept my eyes being different, but question my fangs?" He placed a finger across Lewis's lips before he could answer. "I'm a vampire. I'm guessing that's why my aura is red. I drink blood… animal blood, that is. You're safe with me, I promise."

Lewis's shoulders sagged in relief. "I'm not going mad. That's something… at least." He tilted his head to one side, thoughtful. "Vampire, hmm? You go out in daylight, so obviously, the stories got a few things wrong. Unless you *can* turn into a bat, and you're leaving that titbit of information until I've accepted this first. And where's your coffin? Don't tell me. It's upstairs, yes?"

No wonder Cyrus had never invited him upstairs. A lot of things made more sense now.

A half-remembered story made Lewis catch his breath. "So, are you like Lord Ruthven, or Count Dracula?" Curiosity bubbled out of Lewis. "I assure you I'm no Aubrey, and you'll find my sister isn't one to fall for a man with charm without good reason."

"That's good to know. And you're nothing like Mr Harkness either, I hope. Unless you're hiding your collection of stakes at the boarding house." Was Cyrus teasing or serious? "I must say, you're taking this much better than I expected."

"I'm psi." Lewis shrugged. "I've seen some peculiar things in my life. I'm relieved that my ability isn't malfunctioning. I couldn't work out what I was seeing." He frowned, thoughtful. "Does that mean Victor and Alan are too? Vampires, I mean. Their auras are red like yours."

"Yes, and Elard." Cyrus kissed Lewis's forehead. "You don't know how relieved I am that you're not scared of me."

"Why would I be?" Lewis didn't understand. "You're still you. What you are doesn't change that." He bit his lip. "I was scared you'd feel differently about me once I told you. Having someone believe me is… a nice change."

Cyrus's eyes narrowed. "Did someone try to hurt you because of what you are?"

"No." Lewis squeezed Cyrus's hand. "I've never told anyone before you. My… a cousin told her beau. He tried to convince her to check into Seacliff Asylum and, when she refused, attempted to get her assessed by the hospital. He saw her conversing with ghosts he couldn't see and thought her quite mad. Luckily her parents had a long conversation with the local magistrate and put a stop to the proceedings. She was never the same, though." His voice hardened. "Her former fiancé skipped town shortly afterwards. The last I heard, he was on a ship heading for Australia."

Not all psi powers were as harmless as Lewis's. And their community had always protected their own.

"If anyone does try to hurt you, they'll have to go through me." Cyrus stood and paced. "You're safe here in Kedgetown, and you don't have to hide who you are."

"I'm fine." Lewis patted the sofa cushion next to his. "Come sit. Can I ask you some questions? I'm not scared," he added quickly when Cyrus's expression fell. "Just curious."

"I'm sorry I didn't tell you sooner. I wasn't sure if you'd still want me and… I… I didn't want to lose someone else." Cyrus sat but kept a distance between them. "I'm not contagious. You won't catch anything from me. We can only turn people around the anniversary of becoming a vampire." He hesitated. "That's not for a couple of months yet. Not that I'm planning to turn you or anything. Heaven forbid. Unless you wanted me to, of course."

"I don't know enough to make that decision." Lewis edged closer. "Yet." Although they'd shared their secrets, Cyrus still seemed reticent and a little nervous. Lewis searched his memory for what he'd read about vampires, although he hadn't taken much interest in it. Not like his sister, who had devoured everything she could find on the subject after reading Dr Polidori's story. "Blood keeps you young? I've never stepped out with an immortal before."

Cyrus snorted. "You shouldn't believe too much of what you've read. Most of the myths have been spread by our kind in an attempt to keep us safe. I'm not convinced that was the right approach, but I'm not about to argue with the Supernatural Council. I'm not immortal, although we age more slowly than you do. We drink blood to stay healthy, the same way you eat your vegetables."

"Blood instead of vegetables." Lewis blinked. "I guess that makes sense."

"Or with them," Cyrus added with a smile. "I'm rather fond of my vegetables and other food. Imagine not being able to sample my own baking? He mock shuddered.

The paper in Lewis's pocket crinkled, reminding him of the warning it held.

"You're worried about something." Cyrus's expression instantly darkened. "I thought you'd taken all of this in too easily."

"I am, but it's not about you or what you've told me." Lewis retrieved Louisa's letter and smoothed it out on his lap. "This arrived earlier today from my sister, Louisa. She's psi like me, although her ability is a little different. She gets glimpses of possible futures. They don't always come true. The future isn't set, you see. We can change something of little consequence."

"You don't think whatever this is can be easily altered."

"No." Lewis handed Cyrus the letter, then waited.

Cyrus scanned it quickly, frowned, glanced at Lewis, and then re-read it. "War," he said slowly. "There's another war coming."

"Is that what you think this is?" Lewis hadn't made the connection. Louisa had seen death on a huge scale, of men screaming, limbs lost, along with their sanity. "I thought perhaps a disaster of some kind. An earthquake...."

"I've fought in too many to not recognise what she's describing." Cyrus looked grim. "With your permission, I can share this with Victor. He was a soldier for decades. I was more of a rebel, signing up for whatever I thought would advance the cause."

"Cause?" Lewis asked. "You've used that word before when you told me about Donagh."

"The Irish cause. Taking Ireland back from the British." Cyrus's voice was tight. "I lost him to it, as I told you. In Wexford in 1798." He folded the letters into quarters. "I came here after the 1916 Uprising. Victor and I fought on opposite sides. I couldn't stay with the British hunting me. I couldn't risk surviving something I shouldn't and revealing our kind to the humans. Or them finding out how they can kill us."

"I'm sorry." Lewis suspected nothing he could say would go anywhere near easing Cyrus's pain. He leaned his forehead against Cyrus's. "I had planned to tell you about what I was before we took whatever we have—"

"Love," Cyrus whispered. "What we have is love." He seemed suddenly unsure. "Isn't it?"

"Yes." Lewis brushed his lips against Cyrus's cheek. "As I said, I don't care what you are. Her letter scares me, though. If something bad is coming, how much time do we have? I don't want to lose you and regret what we didn't do. I want memories of a life together, even if it's only for a few months."

"I'm not that easy to kill."

"Yes, but I am." Lewis hesitated. "She telephoned me this morning, too."

"Another glimpse?" Cyrus had gone pale. "If there's a war, you're going to fight in it, aren't you?"

Lewis nodded. "And so are you." She'd seen both of them amongst the carnage, her description of Cyrus too accurate considering they'd never met, and Lewis hadn't a photograph to send her. "Her glimpses are usually only a few months into the future and never longer than a year away. If… when… we don't have long."

"I'm not losing you." Cyrus pulled Lewis close and held him tightly. Lewis leaned into Cyrus's embrace, wishing they could stay safe in each other's arms forever.

Finally, Lewis reluctantly pulled free but held out his hand to Cyrus before he could mistake the intent. "I love you. I want to be with you. I'm yours if you'll have me."

"I love you too." Cyrus captured Lewis's mouth in a searing kiss. "Can… I want to take you to bed. To be with you properly and get a start on making those memories we both want."

"I'd like that too."

Cyrus took Lewis's hand and led him to the stairs.

"You're showing me your coffin?" The question slipped out before Lewis could help himself.

Strong arms encircled him, keeping him safe.

"Stupid myth," Cyrus grumbled. He ran a fang over the tip of Lewis's ear, then whispered. "I have something so much better. A large comfortable bed."

∾

Cyrus led Lewis into the bedroom and closed the door behind them. Once he had Lewis in his arms, he didn't want to be interrupted, and Victor would take the shut door as a clear do not disturb sign.

"You're beautiful when you're aroused." Cyrus closed the gap between himself and Lewis at vampire speed.

"What?" Lewis frowned. "But you were over by the door and…. Oh." His heart sped up, its beat loud to Cyrus's vampire senses. "I feel very privileged to see you as you truly are." He slipped two fingers into the v of Cyrus's jersey and pulled him close.

Cyrus took the invitation, caught Lewis in an embrace and kissed him deep and long. When they broke the kiss, Cyrus reached for Lewis's shirt buttons with shaking hands. "It's been so long since I've been with someone for love," he whispered. "I'm torn between savouring you, and not wanting to wait."

"Why not both?" Lewis smiled, and his eyes twinkled. "I don't know about you, but I'm not planning to have you only once tonight. I've waited long enough. I want to enjoy you in every way I can."

"Definitely both." Cyrus pushed Lewis's shirt off his shoulders, then scraped his fangs across the gap between Lewis's singlet and his neck.

"Oh. My." Lewis's eyes glazed over. "Do that again." He hesitated. "Please."

"Anything you want." Cyrus paused long enough to yank Lewis's singlet off and toss it onto the floor. "Anything."

Lewis backed them towards the bed until the back of his knees hit the wooden frame. "I want to see you," he said hoarsely. "I've dreamed of this moment, and already the reality is so much better."

"You have?" Cyrus quickly undressed and took a step

back, his body heating in response to Lewis's gaze. "I have too."

"So much better." Lewis toed off his shoes, sat on the bed and rid himself of his trousers and undergarments. He made a come-hither gesture with his hand. He shuffled back, then sat with his back against the headboard, his legs stretched out in front of him.

"Exquisite." Cyrus crawled up the bed to sit on Lewis's lap. Lewis's body hair was the same pale shade as his hair, the sprinkling on his chest barely visible.

Lewis flushed. He ran a finger down Cyrus's chest. "Like yin and yang. Pale and dark. I do love a man with plenty of body hair." He caught his fingers in Cyrus's curls, then ducked his head to flip his tongue across one of Cyrus's nipples. "Definitely better than anything I could imagine." He hissed when their cocks brushed against each other. "Make me yours." He swallowed, a shy expression crossing his face. "You're not my first, and I know I'm not yours, but we could pretend. Couldn't we?"

"You're the first man I've loved since Donagh." Cyrus retrieved a jar of oil from his bedside table. "I've waited a long time for you." He dribbled some of the oil onto his fingers. "I've had others, but not like this. Never like this." He slid off Lewis, who spread his legs, inviting Cyrus in.

"Only one other for me. I thought… we were always too scared of getting caught."

"You're safe here. With me." Cyrus didn't want Lewis to experience that fear again. "I promise to be here for you and be whatever you need."

A shadow crossed Lewis's face.

Cyrus shook his head. "We're here together now. The future hasn't happened yet, and we'll face whatever happens together." Lewis's sister hadn't mentioned their deaths. Cyrus would hang onto that thought with everything he could unless something happened to prove otherwise. "Tonight is about the present." He managed a smile. "If you're thinking about anything else, I'm not distracting you enough."

"I'm sor—"

"Never apologise for who or what you are." Cyrus spread the oil over Lewis's entrance, preparing him for their joining. Lewis gasped and gripped Cyrus's hand. "Tonight is about trust. About us."

One finger followed another. Lewis's hole was tight, his cock already dripping pre-come. He made a keening sound when Cyrus stopped touching him. Lewis slid down the bed, taking Cyrus with him.

"I want to see you when you take me. Please." The way Lewis said please sent heat through Cyrus.

He carefully placed the bottle of oil on the table, threaded his fingers through Lewis's, and grabbed Lewis's buttocks, rolling him so they were side by side. "You're beautiful." Cyrus licked down Lewis's shoulder. "I love you." He rubbed their cocks together. "Mine."

"Yours." Lewis kissed Cyrus, his tongue mimicking the rhythm of their hips.

Cyrus pushed inside, cautiously at first, watching Lewis carefully. Lewis hissed, his breathing sped up, his mouth sliding free of Cyrus's lips.

"Yes. Yes." Lewis arched his hips, meeting Cyrus's thrusts. He squeezed Cyrus's free hand.

Cyrus nipped Lewis's shoulder, their movements speeding up. Lewis tightened around Cyrus.

The world around them faded to the two of them.

Cyrus thrust faster, kissed Lewis, and then let go, Lewis's orgasm following a moment later. Cyrus took Lewis in his arms, holding him. "I love you."

Lewis clung to him, then slowly relaxed. "Don't," he whispered when Cyrus started to pull out. "We can stay like this for a moment. Can't we?"

"Whatever you want." Cyrus hesitated, then added, "my love."

"I like that." Lewis smiled crookedly, his eyes bright. "I do feel safe. More so than I have for a very long time. I'm tired of hiding who I am. Too many secrets. My heart doesn't feel heavy now." He stroked Cyrus's brow. "You understand that. You're living with that too." His voice softened. "You must have been lonely on your own for so long. Over a century. It's going to take me a while to process that."

"I'm not alone. Not anymore." Cyrus kissed Lewis's fingers one by one. The first few decades he'd grieved for his lost love. The man who had turned him had taken care of him and given him a good start. But his companionship hadn't filled the hole in Cyrus's heart. "I have friends who are like family, and now I have you." He smiled. "You've lightened my spirit, too."

"Your aura isn't as dark." Lewis bit his lip and looked away.

"What's wrong?" Cyrus cupped Lewis's chin in his hand and turned his head, so they were facing again. "Should I pull out? I didn't hurt you, did I?"

"You can if you'd like, but no, it's not that." Lewis shivered.

"I'll get a cloth to clean us up, and then we can talk." Cyrus hesitated. "Or I can hold you if you don't want to talk about what's bothering you."

"I think I'd like to spend the night in your arms and remember this evening. We can talk later." Lewis smiled, but his eyes were sad. "Your aura isn't dark. You're safe. You'll get through this. You have to."

~

When Lewis woke, the room was dark. Birds sang in the lightening sky, celebrating the dawn of a new day. Cyrus moved in his sleep, curling more into Lewis, but didn't wake. Lewis rested his head on Cyrus's chest, momentarily alarmed by the lack of heartbeat, and then the memory of the evening before flooded back.

Cyrus had accepted Lewis, his peculiar ability and all, although he was obviously concerned about whatever was worrying Lewis. Louisa's letter had troubled Lewis, but being with Cyrus had enabled him to push her words to one side. The change in Cyrus's aura brought everything back, robbing them of the wonderful post-coital glow they could have had.

Lewis wondered what strange and amazing things Cyrus had seen over the years and the places he must have been. Perhaps, when the world was calm again, Cyrus could show him some of them. "I'd like that."

"Like what?" Cyrus put his arm around Lewis, who looked up at him and smiled. Cyrus kissed Lewis tenderly, taking his time. Savouring their intimacy like he'd said he wanted to.

"Sorry, I didn't realise I'd said that aloud." Lewis snuggled into Cyrus, enjoying being close. Neither of them had bothered re-dressing. The tail end of summer brought with it mild nights, and Lewis was glad for the coolness of Cyrus's touch, although his skin had certainly been heated the night before. "I was wondering about all the sights you've seen and thought that maybe one day you could show me."

Cyrus's face lit up. "Travelling is so much better when you have company. I'd love to. We could travel the world together. It would be wonderful."

"You could show me your life. Everywhere you've been." Lewis chewed on his lower lip and propped himself up on one elbow. Not hearing Cyrus's heartbeat was still a little disconcerting, but Lewis would get used to it in time. "I'd love to learn more about who you are too."

"We have plenty of time for that." Cyrus brushed Lewis's hair back from his forehead. "Something's still troubling you." The blanket fell forward when Cyrus mirrored Lewis's position. He ran one hand over Lewis's hip. "Can I help?"

"It's nothing to do with what we did last night. I enjoyed that. I love being with you."

"I didn't think it was." Cyrus pulled the blanket up to their waists. "You're cold. Do you need another blanket? I'm sorry I'm not good for sharing heat." He grinned. "I've been told werewolves are good for that."

Lewis blinked. "They're real too?"

"Oh yes. There are a few in town. You've met several already." Cyrus chuckled when Lewis's eyes widened.

"Annalise from the bookshop and the Fowlers for sure." Lewis finally had his answer about what the other unusual aura in town meant too.

Cyrus raised an eyebrow. "You can see their auras. Of course. So… vampires are red. What colour are werewolves?"

"So, they are werewolves!" Lewis went out on a limb. "Scott is something different. He's the first person I've met that doesn't have one."

"Yes." Cyrus hesitated. "He's been here since the town was founded, but I'm not sure exactly what he is. I've heard rumours over the years, but I haven't been here long enough to find out. If he wants you to know, he'll tell you. You already guessed about werewolves, so I could confirm that."

"I know all about people having their own secrets to tell." Lewis gave Cyrus a reassuring kiss. "Werewolves have two auras, shifting between yellow and orange. I figure the colour depends on what form they're in and whether their wolf is close to the surface or not." He shrugged. "I'd never come across anyone with two auras at the same time before, and I couldn't figure out why."

Cyrus looked pleased. "You have all this figured out. Do psi have their own colour?"

"Purple. Human auras are connected to their personality, or… their… health."

"Last night, you said mine wasn't as dark." Cyrus put his arm around Lewis. "That bothered you. Why?"

"Your heart lightened, and it showed." Lewis looked away. "The last few days, I've noticed some of the townspeople's auras are darkening to the point they're changing colour. Grey. Black." He shivered. "The only time I've seen that is when people are ill. Before…."

"You think it's because of what's coming?" Cyrus's grip tightened. "Can you tell me who?" He spoke urgently. "Perhaps we can warn them."

"You can't change fate." Lewis shook his head and focused on the different colours in the patchwork quilt hanging over the nearby chair. "Believe me, I've tried. Warning someone they're going to die never ends well. It's better not to know your future."

Cyrus grew silent. "What about your own aura? What does that tell you? Is this… war… or whatever it is going to take you from me?"

"I can't see my own aura." Lewis turned to look at Cyrus, wishing he could wipe the fear from his face. "When I was younger, I peered at myself in the mirror for hours, determined to get a hint of something but only managed to give myself a headache."

He'd convinced himself, not knowing his future was for the best. He didn't want to know if he was destined for an early death. Lewis closed his eyes.

Alan. Adam. And at least half a dozen others in town

either weren't coming home or their lives would be irrevocably changed.

"I could turn you," Cyrus said slowly. "I'll be contagious in a couple of months. We could still have time."

"No." Lewis regretted the terseness of his reply when Cyrus recoiled. "I don't care that you're a vampire, but I'm new to your world. It's too soon. I need to find my own way first and figure out what I'm meant to do with my ability." He took a breath. "I want to be able to help with what's ahead, and I'm not sure I'll be able to if I'm like you."

"I've never known a vampire with psi powers, but you might retain them." Cyrus looked hopeful. "I could ask. Elard has a friend who might know. He—"

"I have a path to follow, and so do you." Lewis looked Cyrus in the eye. "Louisa saw us both in the midst of what's coming. Not together, and not dead either. I want to think we have a long life together after this, but we don't have that luxury until this is over." He swallowed, his mouth dry. "I don't want to argue. Please." He'd seen enough of Louisa's premonitions to know the foolishness of fighting anything on this scale. "Let's enjoy the time we have together now."

"Promise me you won't do anything foolish." Cyrus pulled Lewis close and held him tightly. "Whatever happens, I'll wait for you. And if you're too long in coming home, I'll find you."

"I'll wait for you too. And find my way back to you. Whatever it takes."

CHAPTER TEN

"A little to the right."

Mason dutifully took a couple of steps to one side and turned his phone to give Elijah a good view of the wall through AbenChat. "The last of my stuff arrived early this morning." He'd spent the next few hours figuring out where he should hang the painting, finally settling on the wall near his desk.

"That's gorgeous. I love the colours and the way the light of the moon reflects off the waves." Elijah wore a goofy grin when Mason propped up his phone on his desk so they could see each other. "Who's the artist?"

"Umm, that would be me." Mason ducked his head. "I used to paint, landscapes mainly, but I haven't in years." He'd lost his muse after the almost overdose and hadn't picked up a brush since. "I'm considering taking it up again."

"Sorry I couldn't be here to help you organise everything." Elijah had been offered a construction job in Wellington last month and, with his savings running low, couldn't afford to turn it down.

Mason shrugged. "Hey, we both need to work. I'm lucky I

can do it from home. At least now the wi-fi works properly." He'd had a few issues with it until Scott had turned up and saved the day. For a town doctor, the man had a few other talents, even if he wasn't very forthcoming about how or why.

"Last week away, and I'll be home on Saturday for good." Elijah lowered his voice. "Just seeing you on weekends isn't cutting it. I miss you."

"Miss you too." Mason smiled. "I'm thinking of Kedgetown as home now, too."

"Same." Elijah's expression softened. "Not only Kedgetown but you. Being away from you has made me realise how much better my life is with you in it."

"It's not the same without you here."

"Even if I do throw off all the blankets?" Elijah's first weekend home after being away for a couple of weeks had derailed their decision to take things slowly. Since then, he'd stayed with Mason at the house every weekend. The aunties had nodded approvingly and made comments about it definitely being time.

Mason was going to ask Elijah to move in this weekend. Officially, all his stuff had steadily been arriving in a succession of boxes at the B&B over the last week. Although they had exchanged no declarations of love yet, Mason had fallen hard for Elijah over the past few months and didn't want to imagine a life without him.

"I can almost forgive that." Mason chuckled. "Almost, considering the other benefits of having you in my bed."

"Aww. Love you too," Elijah teased.

Mason blew a kiss to the screen, keeping their conversation light and flirty, though his heart sped up. Was it too soon to invite Elijah to move in? Whatever his response, Mason wasn't going to ask over AbenChat.

Sex with Elijah was great, but a fantastic physical relationship didn't mean it was time to put a label on how they truly felt about each other. Did werewolves equate one with the other? Mason still had to remind himself what Elijah was on occasion. He loved Elijah for who he was, and what he was didn't matter.

Should it?

Butterflies fluttered in his stomach. What if Mason was reading everything between them through an entirely different lens?

"I went for a run this morning," Elijah continued. "Can we do that this Saturday if the weather's okay? I prefer running with you. Everything I'm doing, I'm remembering us doing it together, and I miss it."

"Yeah, so am I. I can't wait to see you in person, especially as you couldn't get back last weekend. There's… Mason hesitated. "Are you alone?"

"Yeah, and with as much privacy as possible in a house full of werewolves." Elijah frowned. "What's up? Are you having any problems with your oranges?" He used the ridiculous code word they'd finally decided on to discuss Mason's abilities.

"Apples, I think." Mason wasn't sure why he'd agreed to a fruit-based code, but at least this way, they could discuss Postscript without fear of any eavesdroppers—intentional or otherwise—knowing what they were on about.

"Have the aunties been any more forthcoming about the house? You're not having any regrets about uprooting from Invercargill?"

"Nothing like that." Mason caught sight of something out of the corner of his eye. "Bloody hell, there it is again. Give me a minute." He pushed back his chair, determined to catch the furry interloper, but the upstairs flat was empty. And nothing could reach the stairs that quickly. Nevertheless, he sprinted over to the top of the staircase and peered down before returning to his desk.

"Mason? You okay?" Elijah sounded worried.

"I'm fine," Mason assured him. "I'm beginning to think the house is haunted."

"Oh?" Elijah frowned. "I didn't see anyone when I was there last." He looked thoughtful. "Do you think it might be Lewis?" They still hadn't found out what had happened to him after he'd come back from the war. "What have you seen? Or heard?"

Mason got up and paced across the room, holding the phone in front of him so they could continue their conversation. "Promise you won't laugh."

"Never. Scout's honour."

"You were a scout?" Mason raised an eyebrow.

"No, but the thought's there." Elijah leaned forward, his face filling the screen. "What did you see? Do I need to come home? You don't need to stay there if it's something scary, although, in my experience, ghosts seldom are. They're usually quite chatty, in fact."

Mason blew out a breath. "I think we have a ghost cat."

"Seriously? Wow, cool as." Elijah chuckled. "What does this cat look like?"

"That's the thing. I've only caught glimpses of him… her… whatever. Mainly a bushy tail disappearing around a corner. Yesterday morning I woke to a weight on my feet, but when I opened my eyes, I was alone." Mason stopped pacing and peered out the window onto the street below. "And I've heard purring. He's one contented-sounding cat, which I guess is a good thing. I've asked around, but no one's seen anything, or is leaving food out either."

"Did you leave some food out, in case?"

"Yeah, but nothing touched it."

"Weird. Have you asked the aunties?"

"Total waste of time. They do that smile thing like they know something and then ask if I want more dessert." The aunties insisted on ensuring he was well-fed, despite his assurances that he was more than capable of cooking for himself.

"That sounds about right. I'll see if I can sniff it out when I get back on Saturday. If you don't feel comfortable in the house, you could stay in my room at the B&B."

"Nah, it's fine." Mason felt foolish now for mentioning the cat. "And that's the weird thing. Despite all that, I'm happy to stay here. The house feels peaceful, and I've had hardly any… oranges… either. None here, and only one at the bakery the other day." He shrugged. "And that one was quite sweet, really." He dropped his voice to a whisper. "Mac gave me an old wooden bowl he'd found, which he said belongs to the house. I heard music and saw Lewis and Cyrus slow dancing together. Not in the bakery, though. I think they were here. Upstairs in the flat."

"I guess that makes sense if the bowl came from there." Elijah frowned. "I popped back to the flat to pick up the sweatshirt I forgot this morning and need to head back to work. Weather's still chilly this side of the hill, but I'm not missing the freezing early starts."

"At least it's looking like spring." Mason didn't miss the cold that came with living further south. He glanced at his watch. "I should grab some lunch from the bakery before it closes and get some work in today so I can take some time out this evening."

"You don't want the aunties checking in on you."

"I think they've adopted me." Mason hadn't decided whether he should admit to them yet that he liked the warm feeling that came with that.

"They definitely have." Elijah smiled. "Not sure I'm free to talk after work tonight, but I'll be home in a couple of days."

His tone sobered. "Phone me if anything weird happens, okay? I can be with you in a few hours."

"Okay."

Elijah looked behind him. "Gotta go. Bye."

"Bye." Mason replied to the empty screen. His stomach rumbled. Had it been that long since breakfast? He was relying far too much on the bakery for his lunches. Perhaps he should buy a loaf of bread and make it last a few days. At this rate, he'd need a few runs with Elijah to take off the extra weight he'd put on.

He stuffed his phone in his pocket, grabbed his jacket, and headed downstairs. Damn it, with all the talk about the cat, he'd forgotten to tell Elijah his plans for the shop. He'd have more information to share in another couple of days, and they could make an informed decision together.

If Elijah was interested in going into business with Mason.

God, he had a bad case of second-guessing himself today. He needed to get himself out of that one.

"Afternoon, Mac," he said cheerfully when he walked into the bakery. "Hang on, you're not Mac."

The man behind the counter looked about Mason's age and was slimmer and taller than Mac. "I've heard that a lot today." He grinned. "You must be Mason. Mac said you'd probably be in about now." He held out his hand. "Hello, I'm Adam. I work here occasionally when Mac wants to take a break. He had some family stuff come up unexpectedly, and as I was coming into town anyway…."

"Nice to meet you, Adam." Mason shook hands, noting how cool Adam's skin was to the touch. "Are you local, or?" The journal had mentioned an Adam, but he'd been human, and the name wasn't that unusual.

"I used to be." Adam studied Mason for a moment. "You

remind me of Lewis. I'd know you were family, even if Mac hadn't told me."

"You knew him?" Mason took the crumb Adam offered. "I'm living at Postscript. He left it to me."

"I wondered about that." Adam nodded approvingly. "You and Elijah, hmm?" He laughed when Mason frowned. "Local gossip and Elijah's aunties. Rilla has always loved a bit of matchmaking. You have to look out for her."

"That sounds like the voice of experience." Mason figured Adam must be a supernatural of some kind, given he spoke of Rilla in the present tense.

"I was already married when I met her." A shadow passed over Adam's face. "Anyway...." He brightened. "What can I get you today? I have a lemon muffin put aside for you."

"Please, and a loaf of bread." Mason hesitated. "And maybe you could answer a question for me."

"Sure." Adam glanced at him, then busied himself getting the order ready. "Depends what it is, though."

Mason raised an eyebrow.

"I might not know the answer." Adam placed the order on the counter and added the coffee he'd been preparing when Mason walked in. "No charge. On the house today."

"Can you do that?" Mason didn't want to upset Mac by not paying or having Adam out of pocket for it.

Adam shrugged. "The Lemon Tree is partly mine, so yes, it's fine." He paused. "What do you want to know?"

"There's a cat at Postscript."

"Of course, there is." Adam looked amused. "It's nearly October, and she'll be getting ready to open again."

"How did you know I was thinking of opening the book-shop again?"

Adam chuckled. "I know a bit more than most. Comes with having a share in the bakery." His expression turned more serious. "Have you seen him? Or just glimpses? He's a sweet cat, always has been."

"I'm not imagining him then?" Mason wasn't sure whether he should be relieved, or if the cat's appearance was a sign of something else more worrying.

"No, and don't worry, if he's hanging around, it's because he likes you." Adam gave a nod to someone behind Mason. "And there's my next customer. Nice to meet you, Mason."

"You too, Adam." Mason turned at the doorway, giving Wendy a smile in response to her wave.

"Wordsworth," Adam called after him. "When you see that cat again, his name is Wordsworth."

The trip over the Remutaka Hill had taken longer than Elijah had anticipated. Getting stuck in traffic hadn't helped his mood. By the time he pulled up in front of Postscript, the sun had already set. He hated driving the winding hill road at the best of times, but luckily the last of the light had held out until he'd reached Greytown.

A dim light shone in one of the upstairs rooms. Elijah smiled, imagining Mason curled up on the sofa with a book as he so often did in the evenings. Neither of them spent a lot of time watching television, although they had a couple of shows they followed together. Mason had promised to save the new episodes until Elijah could watch with him.

Home.

Elijah climbed out of the car and retrieved his backpack from the boot. He took a deep breath, savouring the air. Silly as it sounded, he swore the scent here was subtly different.

Magical almost.

Now he *was* being foolish.

Mason wasn't expecting Elijah home until the morning,

but Elijah didn't want to spend another night in a bed alone. He fished out his key and let himself in.

He heard low voices, like a background noise just out of reach. He sniffed, but the only scents were Mason and the barely started corned silverside and golden syrup in the slow cooker.

A strong perfume, sweet with an undertone of honey, filled the air, then disappeared.

Weird. Perhaps it was tied to the ghost cat Mason had mentioned.

Elijah dumped his bag at the bottom of the stairs and sprinted up them.

Mason met him at the top brandishing a cricket bat.

"Whoa, it's me." Elijah held up his hands in mock surrender.

"Sorry." Mason lowered the bat, then pulled Elijah close. "I've missed you." The bat fell to the floor. "So much." He clung to Elijah for a few moments, then kissed him soundly. "You're home early."

"Yeah. I missed you too and thought I'd surprise you." He frowned. Mason was shaking. "You okay?"

"I thought I heard someone in our bedroom earlier." Mason looked sheepish. "I went to take a look, but no one was there." He bent to pick up the bat. "I went to check the front door was locked and found this next to the side table in the hallway. It definitely wasn't there before."

"I heard voices when I came inside," Elijah confirmed. "And I smelt something sweet, like honey. Have you bought any plants since I left?"

Mason frowned. "No. Your aunts gave me a fern and an African violet as a housewarming present, but nothing like that. There are a couple of mānuka trees in the back garden, but they're not in flower yet. I've been working out there a bit in the evenings."

"Do you think it's connected to the cat?" Elijah kept his tone light.

"Wordsworth," Mason corrected. "I met Adam at the bakery. He knew about the cat. And a few other things."

Elijah frowned. "I haven't seen Adam in years, although he does visit Kedgetown frequently. I think he has family here or something. I was going to ask him about Cyrus and Lewis, but figured either I kept missing him or he was avoiding me." He shrugged. "Nice enough guy but no clue what his story is other than he's a vampire."

"He is?" Mason's eyes widened. "I… never mind, it's not important." He seemed to relax. "You're home, and I'm over being nervous and chasing shadows."

"If there are any ghosts here, I'll give them short shrift." Elijah jutted his chin out and struck what he hoped was a heroic pose.

Mason laughed. "Idiot. I think it's more likely my imagination has been in overdrive with you gone. The voices are probably from out in the street, or someone's radio. The night air's really clear. Sound travels."

"Yeah, it does." Elijah kicked off his boots and hung his jacket over the banister. "I can think of a much better way to spend the evening." He paused. "You eaten? I grabbed a pie and chips in Greytown."

"Yeah, although I could do with working up an appetite for dessert." Mason looked Elijah up and down, then licked his lips. "You look great." He leaned in and stole another kiss. "Bed?"

"Fuck, yes." Elijah linked his hand with Mason's and followed him into the bedroom. "Our bedroom?" That's what Mason had called it.

"Yeah." Mason stopped in the doorway. "I want it to be. Not just you spending weekends, I mean. Move in with me?"

He flushed. "Crap, I meant to ask later. After seducing you. Lead up to it and all that."

"You've never needed to seduce me." Elijah caressed Mason's cheek. "I wanted you the first time I saw you, but it took a while for me to realise that."

"Yeah, me too." Mason leaned into Elijah's touch, his fingers already undoing the buckle on Elijah's belt. "Was that a yes?"

"Totally." Elijah undid the top button of Mason's jeans, then the zipper. "Yes. Fuck yes." He rubbed his cock against Mason's, then yanked down both their underwear.

Mason stumbled backwards into the room, pulling Elijah on top of him on the bed. Elijah captured Mason's mouth in a searing kiss. Mason groaned into it.

Elijah broke the kiss and stood long enough to step out of his jeans. Mason's cock stood erect and hard. Elijah swallowed. Fuck, he loved it when Mason wanted him like this.

"Let me," he whispered, not wanting to break the moment. Elijah pulled his t-shirt over his head, then helped Mason out of his jeans and shirt. "You're so hot. And mine."

"Totally yours." Mason raked his gaze down Elijah. "I…" He swallowed. "I love you. Being away from you, I…."

Elijah shushed him with another kiss. "I love you too. I'm yours too." He searched Mason's eyes, wanting to hear the words. "If you'll have me, I don't want to leave you."

"I'll have you." Mason grinned. "But get a move on, will you?"

"Idiot," Elijah said affectionately. He grabbed the lube from the dressing table. They'd not worried about condoms. One of the perks of being a werewolf.

"Ah, but I'm *your* idiot." Mason sounded so happy that Elijah wanted this moment to last forever.

He bit his lip, blinking away tears. All the years of being alone had been worth waiting for the right guy. For Mason.

"Elijah?"

"I love you," Elijah repeated, loving how the words sounded. He shoved his thoughts aside, focusing on Mason. They'd talk afterwards.

He slathered lube over his cock. Mason whimpered, watching Elijah touch himself. Elijah threw him the lube and nearly came, there and then, when Mason squeezed it over his finger, prepped his hole inside and out, and bucked his hips.

Elijah pounced on Mason, rolled them side by side, and entered him, slowly at first, then speeding up, quickly finding their rhythm.

Mason threaded his fingers through Elijah's hair, kissing him frantically. He moaned into Elijah's mouth and hooked one leg around Elijah's hip, pulling him in further, speeding up.

Heat pooled in Elijah's groin. He groaned loudly, their bodies moving together as one.

Mason broke the kiss and bit down on Elijah's shoulder. Elijah lost control, holding Mason close as they both went over the edge.

"Oh God, oh fuck," Mason yelled.

Elijah lifted his head and howled, then collapsed onto the bed with Mason in his arms. He snuggled into Mason, their hearts beating fast, both covered in sweat.

Mason grinned. "I love it when you howl."

"As long as you don't think it's cute." Elijah swatted Mason's buttocks in a lazy motion.

"Nope. Totally not." Mason's grin widened. He kissed Elijah's shoulder. "I love it when you lose it when I bite you, too."

"It's hot. You're hot as." Elijah sighed, contented. He traced a pattern down Mason's arm. "I'm already not looking forward to having to leave you again for the next job." He'd been guaranteed work in Wellington but didn't want to leave Kedgetown anytime soon. "I suppose I could commute. Other people do it."

Mason met his gaze. "About that. I have an idea that might help. I've done some research, and I think we have a good chance of making a good go of it. If you're interested, of course."

"Oh?" Elijah was intrigued by the excitement in Mason's tone.

"Postscript was a bookshop, right? This flat's more than big enough for both of us, so we don't need the downstairs part. I thought about renting it out, but it didn't feel right."

Elijah guessed where Mason was going with his idea. "You want to open the bookshop again?"

"Yeah. A LGBTQ bookshop. Tourists already pass through the area, so they wouldn't mind a small detour. We could do a mail order service too."

"We'd have to check with the town council." Elijah was sure they'd go for it. "But, as the shop's only been closed for eight months, I can't see there being a problem."

"The leftover stock we found in the back room could go on the shelves too." Mason grinned. "Not only that, but there's a small kitchen downstairs. We could talk to Mac at the bakery and see if he's interested in supplying us with baked goods. That way our customers could stop for morning or afternoon tea too. There's only the pub in town, and they serve meals, so we wouldn't be stealing any of their business."

"I think that's a brilliant idea." Elijah kissed Mason's cheek. "You're not going to miss data entry?"

"God no." Mason shrugged. "For the first time in a very long time, I don't feel worried about my ability either. I... this is going to sound crazy, but I feel safe while I'm in this house. Or with you."

"You're sure?" Elijah had faith in Mason. "Whatever happens with your ability, I'm here for you."

"I wouldn't be considering this otherwise." Mason relaxed in Elijah's arms. "This isn't something I've gone into lightly. Promise me you won't either."

"I won't." Elijah was already excited about reopening the shop. Not only that, but it felt right, like he'd finally found what he was meant to do with his life. He yawned. "Sorry, it's been a long day. How do you feel about sharing a shower with me? We can go through your plans in detail in the morning."

CHAPTER ELEVEN

September 1945

"Still nothing?" Victor asked over the telephone.

Cyrus shook his head, although Victor wouldn't be able to see him. "No." Cyrus had flipped the sign on the bakery to closed half an hour before and had been nursing a nearly cold cup of tea in the kitchen at the back of the shop since. "Perhaps he's still on his way home?"

Everyone in Kedgetown who'd fought in the war was home now. Except for those who were lost, with nothing left to send back to their loved ones.

"Have you contacted his family in Invercargill?"

Victor and Cyrus had both had nightmares about what they'd seen in Europe over the past five years, especially when the concentration camps had been liberated.

"I did when I first came home, but I haven't since." Cyrus raked one hand through his hair. "What am I going to say to them? I can't tell them who he was to me."

My lover, a part of me. My everything.

"From what you've said about his sister, she probably already knows." Victor, always the optimist and ready to see the good in everything, had admitted his struggle to keep the faith.

"Yes, but I…." Cyrus sighed. Before the war, he would have baked a new creation to take his mind off everything, but with the rationing and shortages, he had very little flour left after providing essentials for his customers. He took another sip of tea, then discarded it.

He and Lewis had exchanged letters at first, carefully worded in case they fell into the wrong hands. Then, the letters stopped after Lewis was stationed in Italy last year. News of heavy fighting and casualties amongst the New Zealand troops at Monte Cassino had reached Cyrus a short while later. But no one could tell him anything.

Cyrus's dreams were plagued by images of Lewis living the horror he'd dreaded before he'd signed up, determined to do the right thing. Bad enough to see people around you dying, but knowing their fate beforehand and not being able to prevent it…

He shivered, remembering the humans he and Victor had tried to save, and helped to escape, only to lose them to betrayal and murder.

"I have some connections." Victor sounded calm as usual, his grief over the loss of Esmé's only brother well hidden by a stoic exterior, although Cyrus doubted either of them would ever truly put their experiences behind them. "Do you want me to make enquiries for you?"

Cyrus hesitated, torn between wanting to know, and preferring to keep his illusion that Lewis had survived. "I'd appreciate that, thank you." He turned at the sound of someone at the back door. "I'll talk to you tomorrow. Although you don't have to keep telephoning me every day. You have your own life to lead."

"You're my friend," Victor said matter-of-factly. "This is

what friends do. Take care of yourself, Cyrus. Keep your hope alive, and I'll see what I can do."

"Thank you." Cyrus returned the receiver to its cradle and plastered on a smile.

"I made you a card." Audrey skipped over to Cyrus and handed him an envelope. "I wrote your name on the front."

"That's wonderful, thank you." Cyrus took the card and made a show of opening and admiring it. Her father, Adam, still missing in action, hadn't come home yet either.

Harriet placed a bag of groceries on the bench. "I'll cook tonight. You look like you've had a busy day." She had dark lines under her eyes, and he'd heard her crying at night. She'd kept the bakery going and moved into the guest rooms in the upstairs flat at Cyrus's insistence while he'd been away. He hadn't the heart to ask her and Audrey to find other lodgings once he'd returned.

He also knew better than to offer to help her with the meal. She was fiercely independent and keeping busy helped her get through each day.

"Audrey, why don't we go for a walk after you've done your homework?" he suggested. "I can meet you here in about half an hour. I have some work to do in the bakery, so we'll both be ready around the same time."

"I'd like that." Audrey beamed, then ran upstairs, her school satchel jiggling on her shoulder.

"You're very good with her." Harriet smiled. "You're a natural. Both you and Lewis are. She adores both of you."

While Harriet had worked out that he and Lewis were a couple, she had no idea of the supernatural world that existed alongside hers. Cyrus had debated telling her but decided she was already struggling to find her way in a changing world.

Cyrus tilted his head as a way of acknowledgement. Like him, she still spoke of Adam and Lewis in the present tense.

They'd continue to hope until they had proof their loved ones weren't returning.

He bolted into the bakery and sat with his head in his hands. Who was he trying to fool? "I can't lose him. I've left it too late." Damn it. He should have tried harder to convince Lewis to be turned. "Too late."

They might have still had a future that way. Lewis might have survived.

Cyrus shook his head. Being a vampire was no guarantee. It hadn't saved Alan, whose dust lay somewhere in France. Elard had fought alongside Alan, and seen him die, but hadn't shared the details of his death. He'd stopped for a day in Kedgetown to let the town know about Alan, then continued onto Napier with no comment about when he'd return.

Bloody hell. Cyrus needed to pull himself together. Audrey would be coming to find him soon, and he didn't want to upset the child.

He wiped tears from his eyes. Waiting was killing his spirit, piece by piece. He needed to do something. The bakery was in safe hands with Harriet and the Fowler boys.

Tomorrow, he'd talk to a lawyer. Leave the bakery to them. Equal shares to Adam and his family and the Fowlers. Then he'd travel again. First to see Lewis's family. His sister had the sight. If anyone knew where to start looking for Lewis, she would. Cyrus would bring Lewis home one way or another, even if it was only for a proper burial and to give closure to his loved ones.

Someone hammered on the shop door.

"We're closed," he called out.

"Open up!" Scott bellowed. Ignoring him would be a waste of time. Sure enough, the door opened, and he strode in.

"The door was locked," Cyrus pointed out reasonably.

Not that locks, or anything else, had ever stopped Scott once he put his mind to something.

"I have something you'll want to see."

Cyrus kept his expression neutral. "I'm busy wallowing. In private."

"I can see that." Scott's expression softened. He placed a hand on Cyrus's shoulder. "Life will be rough for a while, but it will get better. I promise."

Scott had been nothing but supportive since Cyrus arrived home. While Scott hadn't fought at the front, he'd held the town together after the earthquakes had hit in '42, and been tireless in helping with the rebuilding.

Annalise and Rilla had opened Postscript to those who had lost their homes during that time too, returning from wherever it was they went when the shop was closed. Cyrus had never heard of it being open during winter before, but with the council building demolished in the first earthquake and with it the werewolf safe rooms, everyone had done their bit to ensure a safe alternative was in place before the full moon a few days later.

"Sorry, I shouldn't be taking my grief out on you."

Scott smiled. "That's the thing. We've all lost friends and loved ones, but your Lewis isn't one of them." He handed Cyrus a telegram. "This came for you. I knew you'd want it immediately, so I brought it over myself."

Cyrus grabbed the thin paper and scanned it.

Coming home. On Masterton train tomorrow morning.

He held it to his heart, its short message blossoming hope where he'd thought he'd never feel it again. "Lewis is alive. He's alive." He glanced up at Scott. "Thank you."

Lewis took his time getting off the train. He'd checked the bus timetable in case, torn between hoping Cyrus might be at the station to meet him and not looking forward to the long silence between them on the drive to Kedgetown.

He adjusted the duffle on his back and kept his head down, avoiding interaction wherever possible.

"Lewis?" Cyrus's Irish accent was music to Lewis's ears, yet he didn't miss the uncertainty in the greeting.

"Hello, Cyrus." Lewis risked meeting Cyrus's gaze. He wanted so badly to run towards him and hold him tightly, grabbing the illusion of never having to let go.

But they were in a public place, so he settled for a smile and held his hand out.

Cyrus's grip lingered longer than a polite greeting. They were two old friends meeting after years apart. They could claim that if asked, couldn't they?

"I'm sorry I didn't write," Lewis murmured. "I needed… I had to find myself again first." He hadn't done a great job of that either, but at least he now had enough composure to face the world again or part of it in small doses.

A loud noise echoed through the carpark.

Lewis jumped and glanced around wildly, looking for a bolt hole.

"It's only a car exhaust." Cyrus's tone was low, soothing. "I'm taking you home. You're safe." He opened the door of the truck. Lewis frowned, wondering what had happened to the bakery van. "Fergus is using my van for deliveries, so I borrowed Alan's truck." Cyrus's face shadowed. "He won't be needing it anymore, so I'm using it in the meantime."

Lewis nodded. He'd known Alan wouldn't be coming home before he'd left, but it still hurt to hear it confirmed. He stowed his duffel at his feet and climbed into the passenger side. He'd missed the Wairarapa, and in particular, Kedgetown. Before the war had broken out, he and Cyrus had taken a few day trips and explored the surrounding towns.

"Adam?" His aura hadn't been as dark as the others. Lewis hadn't discovered what it meant but hoped he'd escaped death somehow.

"Still missing." Cyrus started the van and headed home.

Buildings and shopfronts bore the mark of earthquake damage. Lewis studied them silently as they drove past. Mother Nature had added insult to injury by unleashing first earthquakes, and then floods, while so many people were away fighting.

Communities rallied around to help their neighbours, but the area seemed subdued compared to the first time he'd seen it.

He gripped the side of the seat, his knuckles white. Thinking he could return and continue his life with Cyrus was foolish. The town would be grieving and didn't need him adding to that. Lewis bit his lip. His ability was no bloody use if he couldn't prevent injury and heartache. The aura that came with impending death was impossible to change, but he'd thought at first he could make a difference by mitigating some of the injuries.

That hope had been dashed quickly and violently.

"Harriet and Audrey are living with us," Cyrus said. "They have their own area upstairs and won't disturb our privacy."

"I could find lodgings…."

"No!" Cyrus said firmly, his shoulders tense, then shaking. "The bakery is your home. Our home. That hasn't changed. It will never change." He drove in silence for a few minutes, paddocks passing in an unending loop of scenery. "Do… do you still want to be with me? If you need time, I can…."

Lewis squeezed Cyrus's knee. "I love you. The memories we made together helped me while I was away. I… I need some time. I'm not sure how long. I'm sorry."

Talking to Louisa had helped. But it hadn't been enough.

"I'm not going anywhere." Cyrus kept one hand on the wheel and covered Lewis's with the other. "I love you. I'll be whatever you need. Don't worry about us."

"I'm tired. All… my ability took a hammering while I was away. I feel drained on a good day. I'm not sure I can hold down employment either. I don't want to be a burden."

"Don't worry about that. I've made some good investments over the last few decades. I work in the bakery because I enjoy it, not because I need the money."

"I can't let you"

"I'm offering, and it's fine." Cyrus slowed down as they approached the turn-off for the road leading to Kedgetown. "I want to look after you."

"I need to do *something*." Lewis turned away to look out the window again. The distance between houses lengthened, with fewer building dotting his view as they left the outskirts of the town. "Louisa…." He hunted for the right words, unsure whether they existed. Neither he nor his sister had been sure what she'd seen, only that Lewis needed to come home. "She saw us together. We do something good. The more she spoke of home, the more I realised she didn't mean a place. My home isn't Kedgetown."

Cyrus slammed on the brakes and then parked the truck by the side of the road. "You're not staying," he said flatly. "Is this visit about making more memories before you say goodbye?"

"No." Lewis shuffled closer and kissed Cyrus softly. "My home isn't Kedgetown," he repeated. "It's you."

Cyrus leaned into Lewis's embrace, then kissed him again, gently, yet full of love. He wanted more, and the yearning in Lewis's gaze showed he did too, despite not being ready yet. "You're my home too."

~

The closer they got to Kedgetown, the quieter Lewis became. The conversation they'd started died into silence. Lewis's heartbeat slowed to a steady thump as he slipped into sleep.

Cyrus drove slowly, using the time to think. Although he'd seen the effect of battlefield trauma before, seeing it in Lewis brought Cyrus close to tears. His Lewis was a kind, caring man, full of life and lively conversation. Not someone worn out by the effort of talking. Cyrus felt privileged that Lewis had trusted him enough to share the little energy he possessed. Coaxing Lewis back to life wouldn't be easy.

Cyrus was determined to be there if Lewis wanted to talk, but didn't expect him to. He'd provide Lewis with a home and let him decide what he needed, rather than making decisions for him. Treating Lewis like glass wouldn't achieve anything.

They'd find a balance and make it work.

We do something good.

Cyrus wanted to believe that. Lewis needed to make a difference. He'd talked about that several times before he'd left for Europe. He would have managed it somehow.

But at what cost?

Lewis stirred when they pulled up outside the bakery. The sun shone, a light breeze tugging at the trees lining the street, but the streets were almost deserted. A curtain lifted across the road, then fell. Either townsfolk were busy with lunch, or they were giving Lewis time to get used to being back first.

Or a little of both.

"We're home." Cyrus kept his voice low.

Lewis straightened immediately. He looked around, his shoulders tense, then glanced in the rear-view mirror. "I'll never get used to you not reflecting." A tiny smile creased his lips. "I've missed your vampire quirks."

Cyrus managed a chuckle at the familiar phrase, one Lewis had started using in those last months they'd shared. "Welcome home, my love. Welcome home."

CHAPTER TWELVE

"Do you mind if I share your seat?"

Lewis shuffled along to the end of the bench to give Anthony some room. "I see you finally got your seat."

"I think they took pity on me." Anthony gestured to his empty sleeve pinned to the top of his jacket. "Although I like to think it had more to do with the brilliance of my idea. When I come to the park, there's often someone sitting here." He shrugged. "I'm disappointed I didn't get a plaque, but that can wait. I have a few years left in me yet."

Lewis offered Anthony a scone, and they munched in silence for a few minutes. "How do you joke about dying?" He hesitated. "I'm sorry you were injured."

"So many of us were, and not all injuries are visible." Anthony stared ahead as though seeing a memory rather than the empty field. "Humour is better than anger and grief. Although some days it fails miserably to keep either of those at bay."

"At least you try." Lewis had always got on well with Anthony. They'd connected through their love of books but had avoided each other since returning home. Or rather,

Lewis had stayed clear of conversation with Anthony. He'd always been too easy to confide in, although Lewis hadn't told him about being able to see auras. The few people in town who knew about that were aware of who Cyrus was too.

"Depends on my mood. Yesterday I went through the motions. Today it was easier. I'm trying not to predict tomorrow." Anthony shrugged. "Cyrus is happier with you home. He's worried, but not losing hope like he was before."

"I… I had to make a detour first." Lewis wasn't sure why he needed to offer an explanation. Anthony wasn't the type to push.

"I went to see my family before I came here, too." Anthony smiled, but it didn't quite reach his eyes. "Dad died while I was away, and one of my brothers didn't come home. We're better at keeping in touch now. Mum tried to understand, but I'm not sure she does. I don't want to talk about a lot of it."

"Neither do I." Lewis brushed crumbs from his trousers. "I'm not sure reliving what happened through words will help. I… I've lost my equilibrium, my faith in myself. That's going to take longer."

"You've lost your purpose."

"Something like that." Lewis packed the empty scone wrapping into his bag. He'd finished the thermos of tea about an hour ago. "I keep telling myself I need time, but some have more of a luxury of that than others."

Cyrus said he would wait, but how long did they have, really? Cyrus had already lived several of Lewis's lifetimes. Could Lewis expect him to wait for another?

Some days, like today, he was almost himself again, but other times, not so much. Despite wanting to leave the past behind, he couldn't let go of it. People lacked colour, appearing as black and white photos against a background of grey, reflecting their experiences and loss. He tried not to look at people, scared he'd see more death he couldn't prevent.

When he'd left for Europe, in what seemed a lifetime ago, Lewis erected a wall, boarded his emotions up, and nailed it shut. Showing or feeling anything brought the risk of becoming lost. Occasionally, he let minute emotions sneak through a crack, but soon discovered that wasn't a good idea.

He'd heard whispers, while in Europe, of psi being used as weapons. That terrified him even more and fuelled his determination not to tell anyone in his unit what he saw, or what he was. He'd be locked up or worse.

So, he survived each day, got on with the job and watched from a safe emotional distance, while everything that made him feel died inside the prison he'd made himself.

The kiss he'd shared with Cyrus weeks ago had given him hope. He'd felt something that day, a sliver of emotion he'd thought long gone. Lewis still loved Cyrus and wanted to be with him that way, but as soon as they tried, Lewis would retreat into himself.

His life was flat and grey. Like the auras he'd seen of doomed men and women stalked by death.

"I should get back to work." Anthony interrupted Lewis's thoughts. "If you want some company, you know where to find me. I have some new books at the library you might like. I'll put them aside for you. I've missed our chess games, too."

"Thank you." Lewis gave him a nod, then watched him walk away.

Anthony had always been a sweet man. He and his sweetheart were planning a summer wedding but hadn't decided whether they'd settle here or in Greytown. Joyce would be a good fit for Kedgetown. Everyone in town loved her.

Movement in a nearby bush caught Lewis's eye. He

jumped to his feet, his heart racing. He took several deep breaths and counted to ten.

The bush shook, followed by a plaintive meow. Lewis cautiously approached the bush, then knelt on the grass. Green eyes stared back at him. The cat meowed louder.

"You're stuck, aren't you." Lewis crawled closer.

The cat didn't look very old, perhaps a year or so, but past kittenhood. He or she had crawled into the bush and forgotten how to get out. Or was hiding. Lewis could relate to that all too well.

Lewis held out his hand and kept his voice soft. "Come on, kitty. I won't hurt you." He edged closer.

The cat backed up under the bush and pushed itself through the other side. It stared at Lewis as though daring him to come closer.

"Definitely not stuck then." Lewis figured he'd play whatever game the cat wanted. The tabby was a beautiful animal, its long fur different shades of grey. "I bet you're soft, given how pretty you are."

The cat moved forward cautiously, keeping a couple of inches out of reach.

Lewis kept his hand extended, and perfectly still. The wetness of the grass seeped through his trousers, but he ignored it, determined to make friends with the cat.

"Are you lost?" Lewis sighed. "You and me both. You understand that, don't you?" Its head butted against his hand. He dared scratch it, and the cat rewarded him with a loud purr.

The cat looked up at him. Their gazes locked, then after a few minutes the cat looked away but stood its ground.

Lewis scooped it up onto his lap. He stroked its fur and held it in his arms. "You're a good kitty, aren't you? Such a pretty boy. Or girl."

Tears fell from his eyes. The cat settled into his lap, the picture of contentment.

Lewis lowered his head and sobbed.

He was still sitting there with the cat, unmoving, an hour later when Cyrus found them.

"Why don't you sit in the sun with your tea?" Cyrus suggested. He'd set up an old comfortable sofa on the back porch, complete with a blanket.

Barncat had already perched on one end of the seat and was washing himself. He gave Cyrus a look of cat disdain when he and Lewis approached.

"I should be helping out in the bakery." Lewis took the tea, cradling the cup in his hands. "You spoil me."

Cyrus kissed Lewis's forehead. "I'm happy you're home." He glared at Barncat, who looked at him but didn't move. "We need to find a decent name for that cat. Perhaps you could do that while I finish up." He'd left Fergus manning the counter for a few minutes. "I have a couple of those lemon cupcakes you like that we could have with our tea."

Lewis hesitated, then settled next to Barncat, who immediately sat on his lap. He scratched the cat under his chin. Barncat started to purr. "You're sure it's fine if we keep him?" He put his cup down on the arm of the sofa and pulled the cat close to him.

"I think that cat has moved in, anyway." Cyrus smiled at Lewis's protectiveness of the cat. "And given he's settling in here and wouldn't come out of the barn at all at the Fowler's farm, it's better all round. The Fowlers are happy he's found a kindred spirit. He's a skittish thing apart from when he's with you."

"I think that's why we connected," Lewis said softly. "I'm trying, Cyrus, but I… I need time."

"I know, and that's fine. You don't need to explain yourself or apologise for anything to me." Cyrus brushed Lewis's fringe back from where it had flopped over his face and tucked it behind his ear. "We have time. I'm not going anywhere."

The loud bang from the shopfront made them both jump.

Lewis glanced around, his shaking fingers tightening around the cat's fur. "It's nothing."

Cyrus squeezed Lewis's other hand. "I can stay here if you need me."

"It's nothing," Lewis repeated. "You need to go find out what that was. We'll be fine."

"Bloody Mac," Cyrus muttered. "I told Fergus bringing him to work probably wasn't a good idea. I swear that child can't leave anything alone. I'll be back soon. Sit here and enjoy the sun." He paused in the doorway. "If you need anything, call. I'll hear you."

By the time he reached the shop counter, Fergus was chatting amicably to Scott while Mac sat in the corner sucking on a lemon ice block, his nose covered in flour.

Cyrus took several deep breaths. "Are either of you going to tell me what happened? Or do I need to guess?"

"Sorry for the noise." Fergus glanced towards the back of the house. "I hope I didn't give Lewis a fright." He looked upset. "I turned my back for an instant. Mac had a bowl full of flour and had started to sprinkle it over the floor. I dropped the tin without thinking when I ran to stop him."

Mac looked at Cyrus, grinned, and then went back to devouring the ice block.

"The ice block has calmed them both down." Scott greeted Cyrus with a nod. "Good thing I was passing." He had a habit of being in the right place at the right time.

"And with an ice block," Cyrus noted dryly.

"I had one left, and it would be a shame if it went to waste." Scott gestured to the back of the shop. "I've come to talk to Lewis. Both of you, if you have the time."

"I can finish up here," Fergus added quickly. "It's the least I can do. Dad will be here in a few minutes to take Mac home."

"It's fine," Cyrus reassured him. Mac had already done enough damage for the day, and the ice block was keeping him out of further trouble. He was a bright boy, had a kind heart, but got bored easily. "Scott, I've made some tea for Lewis. Would you like some?"

"That sounds wonderful, thank you." Scott smiled. "And perhaps a leftover lemon cupcake if there's a spare."

"Definitely." Cyrus led Scott out to Lewis. "I'll be in the kitchen making more tea."

Although the comment was a reminder to Scott that their conversation wouldn't be private, he was one of the few people Cyrus trusted not to upset Lewis. Others meant well, but they often weren't sure how to take Lewis when he suddenly went quiet and deserted a conversation as soon as it ventured onto a topic he couldn't deal with.

Scott pulled over a stool and sat next to Lewis so they were on the same level. "That cat has settled in well."

"He feels safe with us." Lewis handed Cyrus his cup. "Could you please top mine up too?"

"Of course." Cyrus walked into the kitchen, keeping both men in sight through the window.

"You've been home almost a month now." Scott didn't waste time with any more small talk, although Cyrus doubted the question about Barncat was without reason, either.

"Yes."

"Recovering from what you've been through takes time."

Scott's tone softened. "A battleground is difficult enough in normal circumstances but horrific for someone with your gift."

"It's not a gift." Lewis's shoulders stiffened. "It's a curse."

"It doesn't have to be." Scott glanced over Lewis's head to Cyrus. Whatever he was doing, he needed to get on with it.

Lewis didn't answer for several minutes, but when he spoke, his voice was rough. "You have no idea what I've been through."

"I'm afraid I have to disagree with you there. I thought I could save my family and friends but instead watched them die. I hated myself at first for surviving when they hadn't. It's taken me years to work out that the way to honour them is by keeping my memories of them alive." Scott continued to speak calmly. "They're not truly gone if they're not forgotten."

"Yes, they are. The men who died aren't coming back." Lewis stood.

Cyrus was at his side in an instant. "You don't have to talk about this, my love," he said quietly. "Scott, I'm sorry, but you need to leave."

Lewis shook his head. "Let him finish, Cyrus."

"My people aren't coming back either." Scott studied both of them, his eyes reflecting grief and pain that Cyrus had never seen in him before. "Don't turn your back on your gift, Lewis. You can do a lot of good. You and Cyrus together."

"That's what my sister said." Lewis sat back down again. Cyrus followed his lead. "You haven't come here just to talk, have you?"

"Wise woman, your sister." Scott smiled. "You're right. You can't bring those men back any more than I can change my past. But you can move forward and help others to find their way." He pulled two keys from his pocket and handed one to each of them.

"These are very old." Cyrus turned his over in his hand, then studied Lewis's. "And they're for different locks. I don't understand."

"She needs two keys," Scott explained. "One is always a supernatural, the other a psi."

"Like us," Lewis said slowly. He took both keys and peered at them closely.

"And those before you, and those who will come later." Scott wasn't making any sense, yet a strong feeling of all being right with the world settled around them.

"There's an engraving on the bow of the key." Lewis showed it to Cyrus. "PS, like when you add something at the end of a letter."

"Postscript is also the name of the bookshop. It opens in a few days." Cyrus glanced at Scott, unsure of the connection. "I've always thought it strange that it lies dormant for most of the year."

"There's a good reason for that." Scott nodded slowly. "Lewis needs time to heal and to find himself again. The two of you are well matched, and that cat… I've always thought a bookshop isn't complete without a cat. Yes, I think this will work out nicely all around."

"What will?" Cyrus put his arm around Lewis. "And whatever you're offering, we're not leaving that cat behind." Despite Cyrus's uneasy truce with the animal, Lewis and the cat needed each other.

"You're offering us the bookshop?" Lewis asked. He'd loved the shop before the war, and often spent hours there choosing new books. "But what about Annalise and Rilla?"

"Talk to them about it. They'll tell you the details, but I'm certain you'll find the offer to your liking." Scott stood and shook both their hands as though they were sealing a deal they hadn't agreed to yet. "Don't worry, I'll see myself out. You'll get all your answers tomorrow." He nodded slowly.

"And this is an offer, one you're free to take or turn down and leave whenever you wish. Good afternoon, gentleman. I'll look forward to your answer once you've fully considered the proposition."

Lewis turned to watch him go, then kissed Cyrus on the lips, leaning into his embrace. "I've always wanted to be a part of a bookshop." Barncat retreated to the end of the sofa and watched them both warily.

"Let's find out the details first, hmm?" Cyrus cautioned, although he already suspected what their answer would be.

"If we decide to do this…." Lewis sounded thoughtful. "I have a name for our cat, a name suitable for a bookshop cat."

"And what would that be?" Cyrus teased, relief flooding through him at the glimpse of the Lewis he remembered.

"Wordsworth," Lewis said firmly. "His name is Wordsworth."

CHAPTER THIRTEEN

"That's it?" Mason took the journal from Elijah and flipped through the blank pages to the back cover. He shook it, hoping for some kind of clue to fall out, but no such luck.

"You did that last time," Elijah reminded him.

"Well yeah, but the pages we've just read were blank then, too." Mason frowned, closed his eyes, and focused his ability. "Typical that I can't get a vision the one time I need to."

"At least that last entry implied they were here in Post-script at some point." Elijah threaded his fingers through Mason's hair. "But..." He hesitated before continuing. "... I'm wondering if they ever left."

Mason snuggled into Elijah. The late afternoon sun streamed through their living room window, and he didn't want to move. One of Mason's favourite ways to spend an afternoon was lying on the sofa with his head on Elijah's lap. "Is that because I've seen Wordsworth's ghost?"

"I'm not sure he is a ghost." Elijah's fingers stilled. "They had a key each like we do, and we're a supernatural and a psi."

"Not *like* we do." Mason slowly put the pieces together. "Those keys *are* our keys, right? The house, shop, whatever, wouldn't have a lot of spares hanging around, especially given how old they look." He eased out of Elijah's embrace and got to his feet. "I'm going to grab them."

"Do you think they hold some clue as to what happened all those years ago?" Elijah stretched after Mason moved off him, the bottom of his T-shirt riding up.

Mason swallowed. "You expect me to stay focused when you do that?" He loved running his hands and tongue over Elijah's skin. "You're so hot," he murmured.

"Well, duh, I'm a werewolf." Elijah joined Mason, kissed his cheek, and followed him to the table at the top of the stairs and the basket where they kept their keys. "We're due at the aunties for tea soon, so we shouldn't start something we don't want to finish."

"I'm in for a quickie if you are." Mason retrieved the keys and handed one of them to Elijah. "Okay, that's weird, and I never thought of it before. You know how the blades are different? That's how we know which one's which."

"Yeah. So?" Elijah held his up to the light. "Mine still looks the same. Cool design, but nothing weird about it."

"I've been working on focusing my ability like we've practised." Mason smiled at the memory of the hours Elijah had spent helping him to hone his ability and gain more control. He closed his eyes and, at the same time, traced the indentation of the PS on the key. "Yours has a slightly different vibe than mine. Mine reacts more to my ability, but it's like yours… complements and focuses it." He looked up at Elijah. "That's crazy, right?"

"Maybe not." Elijah placed the keys side by side on the table. "I took yours by mistake last week, and the door wouldn't open for me. At least not the first time. I jiggled it a bit, hoping you were home, and then it did." He bit his lip, chewing on it thoughtfully. "I thought of you, and the key worked. Perhaps you're the P for psi and I'm the S for supernatural."

"I don't feel so crazy now."

"Because I'm crazier?"

"This whole situation is weird." Something sharp dug into Mason's ankle. "Ouch. What the fuck?" He reached down to wipe the pinprick of blood. The cat at his feet backpedalled, then ran and jumped onto the windowsill.

"That's Wordsworth," Elijah said quietly. "First time I've seen all of him. He looks… real."

Wordsworth studied both of them. His ears pricked up, then he settled on the window, staring out at the back garden. He started to purr.

"That scratch felt bloody real too." Mason edged over to the window, determined to make friends with the cat. "Come on, boy. Where did you come from, hmm?"

An unfamiliar voice called from the bedroom door. "Wordsworth! There you are. Come here, kitty."

"Who's there?" Mason turned in time to see Elijah sprint to the door.

"Where are you?" Elijah sniffed the air, his brow furling. "I know you're there." He entered the bedroom. Mason followed him in. "No one there now, but for a moment, I swear I caught a scent of vampire."

Wordsworth meowed, brushed past Mason's ankles, then faded from sight.

"Shit." Mason grabbed Elijah's hand and squeezed it. "Did you see that?"

"Yeah. What the fuck is going on?" Elijah seemed more curious than scared. "You okay to come back here tonight? We could stay in the B&B and figure out what's going on in the morning if you like."

"This is our home." Mason's voice shook. He cleared his

throat and raised his voice. "We're not moving, okay? Find somewhere else to haunt."

"It's not so bad living with ghosts. I shared a flat with one for a while. She was a bossy shit, but once we came to an agreement about the definition of privacy, we got on well." Elijah kissed Mason's cheek. "But if you want to head out now, that's fine, too."

"Only because I'm hungry, and your aunt is an amazing cook." Mason shrugged, relaxing again now Wordsworth had gone. "Does this kind of stuff happen often?" Every time he thought he was getting a handle on the supernatural thing, stuff like this proved he'd only experienced the tip of the iceberg.

"It's a little out there, even for us." Elijah grabbed his hoodie from over the chair and shoved on his sneakers. "Supernaturals, I mean." He handed Mason his sweatshirt. "This reeks of magic, but I don't have much experience in that. I'd ask Scott, but that would be a total waste of time."

"Maybe your aunts will know." Mason shrugged on his sweatshirt, then found his boots. "Lewis and Cyrus took over the shop from them, right?"

"Yeah, but they haven't been exactly forthcoming with information so far." Elijah sighed. "Worth a go, though, I figure. You ready?"

"Sure." Mason glanced around their bedroom once more, although he didn't expect to see anyone. "Vampires have a distinct scent?"

"Blood," Elijah confirmed. "Unmistakable, even if they haven't fed recently." He waited for Mason to finish zipping his boots. "That's the thing, though. If the vampire is a ghost, I wouldn't be able to smell him. Or her."

"Wordsworth is Lewis's cat, so it makes sense that he would have been the one calling him. I would have recognised Cyrus's voice, and his accent." The vision at the bakery months ago had been Cyrus, Mason was certain of it. "But if Lewis *is* here, Cyrus will be with him. I know how crazy that sounds, but it's the only thing that makes sense. That last journal entry was decades ago. Lewis would be an old man by now unless Cyrus turned him." He drew the bedroom curtains and then headed for the stairs. "That doesn't explain Wordsworth, though. Vampires don't turn cats, do they?"

"Only humans, as far as I know. So, they're not ghosts, but something else. Perhaps an afterimage of something that happened years ago? But I wouldn't be able to smell that either, unless it's like whatever caused that honey scent a couple of weeks ago. Your guess is as good as mine." Elijah reached for his key. "What the fuck?"

Both keys glowed for a moment, bathed in a soft white light, and then disappeared, leaving no trace they'd ever been there.

Elijah knocked on the door of the B&B but let himself in without waiting for someone to answer. The aunties had never worried about locking the door and told him he didn't have to wait to be invited in because he was family.

Mason hadn't been happy leaving Postscript unlocked, and it had taken a while to persuade him that Kedgetown was one of the few places left where it was safe to do so. In a town full of supernaturals and psi, anyone foolish enough to attempt a break-in wouldn't do it again. Besides, Elijah doubted whether they'd have any luck finding spare keys, and the closest locksmith was hours away.

"Interesting," Elijah murmured when he stepped over the B&B threshold. "Looks like we have an extra for dinner."

"Damn it," Mason murmured. "I wanted to ask your aunts about the keys."

"In here," Rilla called from the kitchen.

Elard smiled and stood when Mason and Elijah entered the room. "It's wonderful to see you again, Elijah. It's been a while, yes?" He nodded towards Mason. "And you must be Mason. I'd recognise you anywhere."

"Recognise me?" Mason looked confused.

"Mason, this is Elard, an old friend of the family. Elard, Mason, my boyfriend."

"My apologies. I should have introduced myself first." Elard held out his hand and shook Mason's. "You look a lot like Lewis, but I suspect you've been told that before."

"You knew Lewis, didn't you? And Cyrus." Mason let go of Elard's hand and helped himself to his usual seat at the table. He sounded nervous, and kept glancing at Elard, then away.

"You're his first vampire," Elijah explained. "Or rather, the first he's talked to knowing what you are."

"We're not that easy to spot, but that's kind of the point." Elard chuckled. "I assure you I don't bite, and most of what you've heard about us is nothing more than convenient mythology." He took a sip of what looked like red wine. "But I'm presuming Elijah has already filled you in on all that."

"Yeah, mostly. Actually, not that much. More about were-wolf stuff and all that." Mason flushed. "I'm sorry. I didn't mean to be rude. I've heard a lot about you from Elijah and from Cyrus and Lewis." He paused and glanced at Elijah, who nodded, guessing what Mason was about to say.

"Elard knows about Kedgetown and most of its secrets," Annalise said. "Whatever you wanted to speak to us about this evening, it's safe to include him in the conversation, too."

"I'll help where I can," Elard confirmed. He seemed sad and more reserved than usual.

"We've lost the keys," Mason blurted out. "The keys to the house disappeared in front of us before we came over."

"That's not losing them, dear," Rilla said. "And given that the shop is opening tomorrow, I'd be surprised if you still had them."

"We're not opening the shop for another couple of weeks," Elijah corrected. The stock they'd ordered had been delayed, so they'd decided to wait for it rather than open with half-empty shelves.

"The shop has always opened on the last day of October," Annalise added. "Bright and early, so you'll need a good night's sleep."

"You owned it before Lewis and Cyrus moved in." Mason reached for the teapot in the middle of the table, helped himself to a cup of tea, then poured one for Elijah. "Anyone else want a cup?"

Annalise shook her head. She already had a drink, her favourite brandy, given the scent. "We didn't own Postscript. We were caretakers, like those dear boys."

"I'm happy with my red, thank you. It's been a long day." Elard dabbed his lips with a serviette.

"That's not wine, is it?" Mason handed Elijah his tea.

"Of course not." Elard nodded approvingly. "We were reminiscing and remembering happier times. Unfortunately, my visit isn't just a social one. I've come to pass along some sad news."

"I'm sorry." Mason reached across the table for the milk. His breath hissed when his fingers brushed the side of the milk jug that usually sat in Annalise's china cabinet. She'd brought out the matching Wedgwood dinner set too, which she usually reserved for special occasions.

"You okay?" Elijah recognised the outward sign of a vision immediately.

Mason nodded. "I think this jug was a present from an

old friend," he said slowly. "I don't recognise him, but he feels familiar."

"I've met a few psi in my time," Elard said softly, "but never one with your gift. It's quite remarkable." He took another sip of blood. "Annalise tells me that you've read Postscript's journal, so you'll know Victor from it. He was a good friend to many, and to this town. I wanted to tell Cyrus and Lewis in person rather than have them hear about his death second-hand."

"But they were in the shop decades ago." Mason frowned. Elijah squeezed Mason's knee under the table.

"Yes, they were." Elard cleared his throat. "Because of recent events, we also have two new councillors. I'm sure they'll introduce themselves in time. The new werewolf councillor doesn't have ties to the Waylands, so I'm expecting we're in for some interesting times."

"That's… unusual." Elijah didn't remember a time when the Waylands didn't hold power through the Wellington werewolf council seat. He also recognised deflection when he heard it. They wouldn't get any answers tonight either, so they might as well enjoy the company and the evening and not stress about it.

"No, it's not." Elard showed a hint of fang. "Hedley Wayland finally has someone who is prepared to question him, and not follow the party line."

"Did I miss the local body elections?" Mason looked confused. "Wait, you're not talking about that council, are you?" Elijah had explained to him about the Supernatural Council and its triad of vampires, werewolves, and humans.

"Victor made some progress when he was a councillor, but it's difficult when certain individuals make it their business to block anything new." Elard rolled his eyes. "Unfortunately, not all supernaturals are as enlightened as some of us. However, I'm sure Mr McKenna and Professor

Hawthorne will shake things up substantially. I'm looking forward to it."

~

"The supernatural council is very political." Elijah broke the comfortable silence between them once they were out of earshot of the B&B. "You want to avoid them if you can."

Mason squeezed Elijah's hand, enjoying the warmth of his skin now the evenings were warm enough that they didn't need gloves. Sleeping next to him was like sharing a bed with a hot water bottle that never got cold.

"Most councils are." Mason paused his step to glance up at the night sky. He loved looking at the stars at night. They reminded him of the vastness of the universe and hinted at what else might exist out there that he didn't know about. Coming to Kedgetown had been an eye-opener, but it helped to make sense of his life. "It's wonderfully clear out tonight. Do you want to take our coffee out on the upstairs deck? We could do some stargazing before bed."

"I'm enjoying the view right now." Elijah briefly brushed his lips against Mason's. "I still can't believe I feel so settled here with you. I thought I'd never find somewhere I wanted to truly call home."

"Being with you is home." Mason's cheeks heated. "God, that sounds corny as, doesn't it? That doesn't mean it's not how I feel, though. You complete me, and not only that, but I can be myself with you. Even if my ability does cause trouble, I know without a doubt you have my back, so I'm not scared of it anymore."

"That's exactly how I feel, too. About being home, I mean." Elijah hesitated. "What did you see when you touched the milk jug? You don't have to tell me if you don't want to."

"You can ask me anytime. It's always been easier if I have

someone to talk to about my visions." Mason smiled. "Despite Victor's passing, what I saw wasn't sad. He and his wife were happy, and they'd chosen the jug together. I saw her through his eyes and felt how much he loved her. A tinge of sadness perhaps as well." He bit his lip, his vision a reminder of his future with Elijah. "They only had limited time together. She was human. He wasn't. I guess that will be us one day. Werewolves live much longer than humans."

"We can all die before our time. I might have a potentially longer lifespan than you, but that doesn't mean I will get to live all of it." Elijah turned towards Mason and cupped his face in his hands, caressing Mason's cheek. "I love you, and we're together. That's what matters." He grinned. "Besides, look at the aunties. Death didn't slow Rilla down in the slightest. I expect to be haunted by you for the rest of my days. We'll make it work."

"I'll come back to haunt you, all right," Mason promised. "Don't you worry about that." He kissed Elijah, slow and deep, not worrying about who saw them. When he broke the kiss, they were both breathing heavily. "Hold that thought. I want my coffee on the deck first and to talk for a while." He kept his voice light.

Elijah wasn't fooled for an instant. "Something's bothering you. And not what we just talked about, either." He sniffed the air when he opened their front door. "I might prop a chair under the door handle in case anyone gets any idea about calling in during the night."

"You weren't worried about leaving it unlocked when we left," Mason reminded him.

"The house smells different. Odd." Elijah shrugged. "I can't put my finger on it, but I want some warning if someone's lurking around who shouldn't be." He strode over to the bookshop counter and sniffed again. "No one in the house but us."

"Good. There's not much point barricading ourselves in if there's already someone in here."

Having supernatural families on either side made for a bloody good Neighbourhood Watch. If something went down, they'd have no problem getting in to help, either.

"I caught a human scent." Elijah frowned, scratched at his beard, then shrugged. "All this talk of the shop opening tomorrow has me on edge, I guess. Whatever the aunties know, Elard's in on it. He's always been harder to read than them."

"Practise?" Mason suggested. "How old is he anyway?" Elard looked to be in his mid-thirties, so about their age, although the vision Mason had seen of his spoon suggested the vampire was way older.

"I'm not sure. He doesn't talk a lot about his past, so I've never asked. He was around when the town was founded in the 1800s. He and Scott go way back."

"He's always been a priest?" Mason couldn't get his head around a vampire priest, despite assurances that most of the mythology around vampires wasn't true.

"For as long as I've known him. He moves around the country, so he doesn't stay in one place long enough for anyone to notice him not aging. A lot of vampires do that." Elijah followed Mason up the stairs and leaned against the kitchen counter while he made coffee. "We do as well, to a lesser extent. I believe there are a few places where you don't have to. Some sort of understanding. We protect humans from the nasty things, and they turn a blind eye kind of thing. I don't know where they are, though."

Mason grabbed a couple of cups from the cupboard. "Do you want to stay here tonight? If the shop is opening in the morning, and not by us, do we want to be under its roof? What if some kind of weird shit is about to happen?"

"I'm sure it is. The weird shit, I mean." Elijah took the

cups from Mason. "I'm fine with staying. Curious to find out what the fuck is going on, actually. I've had enough of being in the dark. But if you're on edge and want to leave, I'm with you. Whatever you want to do. Your call. We're in this together, and it's your house."

"I'm not sure it is *my* house." Mason settled onto a bar stool while Elijah took over making their coffee.

"Lewis left it to you." Elijah frowned. "Do you think it wasn't his, either?"

"Annalise said she and Rilla, like Lewis and Cyrus, were caretakers. The last journal entry said Scott offered it to them, so I wonder if he's the owner and Lewis was acting on his behalf." Goosebumps crawled up Mason's neck. He shivered. "Let's take our drinks and go outside, hmm?"

"We're staying then?"

"Yeah. I'm sick of all this lack of explanation and weird comment bullshit too." Mason left Elijah to finish up and headed for the French doors leading outside to the deck. Whatever had changed with the house tonight made him uneasy, but not scared. He'd always been fascinated by the unknown but wary of it too. His ability had taught him the need for the latter all too well.

Something brushed against his legs. Wordsworth meowed, then walked over to the door. The cat seemed more solid than usual. When Mason crouched down, his touch met with long soft fur.

"You're real, aren't you, kitty?" Mason fussed over the cat, earning loud purrs of approval. "Halloween's not until tomorrow night, or I'd be blaming that for this. But you're not really a ghost either, are you?"

"I see we have a visitor." Elijah handed Mason his coffee and then opened the door. "Shit. What?"

"Elijah?" Mason joined Elijah immediately. "What the hell?"

Instead of the long stretch of garden he'd expected, a nature reserve met his gaze. A cobbled path led to a stream, with a bridge leading to a huge grassy area dotted with mānuka trees covered in white blossoms for as far as he could see. Not only that, but instead of darkness, the area was illuminated by the soft light of a dying day. The sun that set hours ago in the world they'd left behind on the other side of the door, was still going down wherever this was.

"This wasn't here when we left." Elijah gestured to the swing seat to their left. "That seat wasn't either."

Mason walked out onto the deck. "There's an outside bath here, too. Not that I'm complaining, as it's really cool." He took a breath, then ran one hand over the wooden seat. "I'm not getting anything from this. Only an echo of something peaceful. Meant to be." If he'd thought they were any danger, he'd take Elijah and leave. Losing his inheritance be damned.

"But it shouldn't be here." Elijah shook his head. "This is seriously weird. It's not like someone's only done a magical makeover of our backyard. There's tons more space than there was before too."

"Maybe we're looking at some kind of pocket universe." Mason couldn't think of any other explanation. He glanced behind them, but apart from Wordsworth sitting on their sofa washing himself, nothing looked out of the ordinary.

"It's bloody magic. It has to be." Elijah didn't look impressed. He raised his voice. "Whoever's behind this, come out and show yourself." He lowered his tone. "Do you think the aunties added something to that last pot of tea?"

"I don't think your aunts are responsible for this, although if they know about it, and I think they do, they wouldn't send us into danger. I trust them, don't you?"

"Yeah, I do." Elijah sighed. "They've always protected me.

You're right. They wouldn't have sent us back to the house if it was dangerous."

Mason breathed in the fresh night air. "I can smell honey, like that evening you came home from your last job away. Given all those trees, that makes sense, but I swear the mānuka in the back garden aren't in bloom yet. Or at least they weren't earlier today." He breathed out, then in again. "I like this. I don't understand it, but it feels right. Don't you feel it too?"

"I guess so." Elijah leaned against the deck railing and surveyed their new surroundings. He cradled his coffee in his hand. "Sorry for my reaction. I don't like things I don't understand. You still want to stay here tonight?"

"Yeah." Mason put his arm around Elijah. "This could be all gone by morning. Let's enjoy the view while we can."

"Until we've finished our coffee." Elijah leaned into Mason. "But before we go to bed, I'm going to grab my phone and take a photo, so we have some proof we're not losing our minds."

"Good idea. If this weirdness was part of our future, of staying in the house, it wouldn't be so bad, would it?" Mason peered out into the fading light. "If this is still here, I vote we explore in the morning." His fingers itched for a sketch pad and pencil. "I want to see all of it."

"You're hot when you're excited." Elijah ran his tongue down Mason's neck. "You're right. If this stays with the house, it wouldn't be a bad thing. Kind of cool, actually. Our own private piece of paradise."

"I like that idea. Of having somewhere that's just ours. Magic or not, let's deal with it in the morning." He yawned.

Elijah took Mason's cup, balanced it on the railing, then caught his mouth in a low, slow kiss. Mason groaned and threaded his fingers through Elijah's hair. They broke the kiss and shared a smile.

Whatever this was, it could wait. Mason suspected it would still be there in the morning. Elijah hooked his fingers through Mason's belt, tugging at it.

"Speaking of private pieces of paradise," Elijah murmured. "It's time for bed."

CHAPTER FOURTEEN

Elijah rolled over in bed and flopped his arm over Mason. Whatever the time, he had no intention of facing the world yet after their late night before. He made a contented noise and snuggled into the blankets.

Water ran in the bathroom.

He creaked open one eye, his vision hidden by the white-blond hair spread out on the pillow next to his. He took a deep breath, inhaling Mason's scent—

What the hell? Elijah backed up, and rolled onto the floor with a thud.

"What the fuck?" Mason yelled from the bathroom at the same instant, Elijah realised the man in their bed wasn't Mason.

The man sat up and rubbed his eyes. He glanced at Elijah, then pulled the blankets up over him. "Bloody hell. What are you doing in our bed?"

"*Our* bed." Elijah growled. He grabbed at the blankets. "Lewis? How are you here?"

"You're not having those!" Lewis looked so like Mason, they could have been twins. "Not until I'm dressed!"

Suddenly, a dark-haired man stood next to Elijah, seemingly appearing out of thin air. His eyes turned fully black, and he dropped his fangs. "Get away from my husband!"

A sharp whistle sounded from the bedroom door. Mason dropped his fingers from his mouth when everyone froze and turned to look at him. He had a towel wrapped around his waist, his hair dripping water onto the floor.

"That's better. Cyrus and Lewis, right? I'm Mason. This is Elijah." Mason seemed more surprised than afraid. "I don't get it. You look the same, but it's been decades." He glanced at Elijah. "Is Lewis a vampire too?"

"Not yet," Cyrus said softly. He seemed to relax. "My apologies for my reaction. I didn't recognise you at first. When I left our bed, our surroundings looked very different."

"Yes. I'm Lewis, and this is my husband, Cyrus." Lewis gazed at Elijah, then Mason, his attention lingering before he turned his attention to the bedroom. "You've redecorated."

"We live here," Elijah pointed out. He grabbed his jeans from the floor by the bed and yanked them on. Being a werewolf, he usually wasn't bothered by being naked in company, but dressing gave him a moment to recover his composure.

"So do we," Lewis said mildly. He reached for Cyrus's hand and squeezed it. "Postscript opens today. You're the new caretakers, so she takes on your reality, not ours."

"We are?" Elijah frowned. "We're opening the shop in a couple of weeks if that's what you mean. Still doesn't explain what you're doing here, though." He crossed his arms and glared at the vampire in his space.

Cyrus backed up enough to sit on the bed next to Lewis. "Time moves a bit differently in the other place." He ran his thumb over the back of Lewis's hand. "Sorry. We knew you'd be here, but we got a little, er… distracted last night. I thought we had a few more days before your arrival."

"Perhaps we could discuss this over breakfast?" Lewis

suggested. "I'm famished, and I could do with a decent cup of tea."

"Sure." Mason grabbed his clothes. "We'll finish dressing in the bathroom and give you some privacy. See you in a few."

"Okay." Elijah followed Mason into the bathroom and shut the door behind them. He kept his voice low despite Cyrus being able to overhear their conversation if he wanted to. "What the fuck, Mason?"

"Bloody hell." Mason looked shaky now they were alone. "That's Lewis and Cyrus. They've been here the whole time? In our house, and the shop? But why didn't we see them before now? Lewis looks the same. How is that possible?"

Elijah pulled Mason into an embrace and held him tightly. "I don't know," he whispered. "I don't think they're a threat."

"You were acting like they were before."

"It's not every day I wake up in bed with someone else," Elijah growled. "Fuck it, I thought Lewis was you."

"If it makes you feel better, I don't think Cyrus was happy about you being near Lewis, either." Mason frowned. "They're married? When did that happen? Where the hell have they been all this time?"

"Here, apparently." Elijah finished getting dressed, then tried to wrap his head around everything. "This is giving me a headache." He hated magic for a good reason. Although he'd heard the theory it was advanced science, he'd never been able to connect the two. One made sense and had reason behind it. The other… well, it was magic, wasn't it?

"You and me both." Mason pulled on his t-shirt, then finger-combed his hair. "Cyrus said he recognised us." He shivered. "That kind of creeps me out. At least there are photos of Lewis, and I've seen Cyrus in a vision, but how do they know who we are?"

"Werewolves photograph. Vampires don't. At least you were able to recognise Cyrus from your vision." Elijah leaned back against the wall and tried to get his thoughts in order before they met their guests. Or were they the guests? Maybe he shouldn't be thinking too hard about any of it.

A scraping noise against the closed door was followed by an impatient meow.

"Wordsworth!" Lewis called the cat away from the door. He'd been the one calling Wordsworth the first time the cat had appeared.

Puzzle pieces started to fall into place, but Elijah wasn't sure he liked the picture they made.

"I can hear you thinking from here." Mason slipped his hand into Elijah's and kissed him softly on the lips. "I vote for hearing their explanation as nothing my mind comes up with makes sense."

"I'm worried it *is* making sense," Elijah muttered. He let Mason lead them out of the bathroom.

Lewis looked up from the kitchen. He'd put the kettle on the stove to boil and was looking through the cupboards. "I can't find a teapot."

"We use tea bags." Mason found an assortment of boxes. "English Breakfast, Earl Grey, Ginger and Lemon, or Kawakawa. Take your pick."

"Heathens." Cyrus chuckled. "I hope you're not planning to serve tea bags in the shop. We have a reputation to maintain."

"It's not ours now." Lewis shot Cyrus an amused look. "Whatever they decide to do with it is up to them. Each caretaker reinvents it. Unless you would have preferred we kept Annalise and Rilla's preferences? Everyone loves your baked goods."

Cyrus mock shuddered. "You have a point. Baking and books go well together."

"Your baking goes with everything, my love." Lewis made tea, then led Cyrus over to the table. "This isn't our kitchen, so we'll wait over here. My husband has definite ideas about how kitchens should be set up. It's the baker in him."

Mason laughed, and then he and Elijah worked quickly to put together an assortment of toast and spreads.

"So…" Elijah got to the point when they joined Cyrus and Lewis at the table. "What the hell have we walked into? Exactly? And how do you know who we are?"

Lewis and Cyrus exchanged a long glance.

"Postscript isn't an ordinary bookshop," Cyrus said at last. "She offers hope and refuge to those who need her, caretakers and customers alike. After the war, my Lewis needed a safe space to heal and time."

"Postscript gave us that, and more." Lewis bent to pat Wordsworth. "We've helped so many people while we've been here, but the last year felt like it was finally time to return to our lives."

"But you still look the same." Mason frowned. "You're my nana's brother, yet you look my age. How is that possible?"

"I missed most of Louisa's life," Lewis said softly. "She is one of my regrets, but nothing is without cost. I couldn't have survived without the shop, and she knew that. She got glimpses of possible futures, and she'd seen us talking to you, although her visions didn't usually reach this far into the future. I didn't understand who you were until about a month ago. The barrier between this world and the one we inhabit while the shop is closed thins closer to opening time. I recognised you from her description, but I didn't know who you were."

"Caretakers only age when we leave the shop or its world." Cyrus took up the explanation. "It's only open between the end of October and the beginning of February, as that's when its magic is at its height."

"So what happens to you when she's closed?" Elijah didn't like where this was going.

"We're here, but not here." Lewis pushed back his chair to let Wordsworth jump on his lap. "When the shop is closed, another world opens up to us. I think you got a glimpse of it last night. That's why the caretakers are a couple. Months alone are a burden for most. I never minded being here with only Cyrus for company. He's my home. He's always been enough."

"Elijah is my home, too," Mason said slowly. "So… you're leaving, and Postscript needs new caretakers?"

"Exactly." Cyrus nodded. "She always provides when it's time to move on." He smiled. "We'll stay for a few weeks to help you find your feet, and then we'll return to the moment we first took on the role."

"One proviso," Lewis added. "You can't change the past. I can't go to my dear Louisa or return to Kedgetown until we get to this moment." He turned to Cyrus. "What did Scott call it again?"

"A paradox."

Mason stood at the window, watching people in the street below. Wordsworth lay stretched out on the sofa, basking in the sun, the picture of a contented cat. Cyrus and Lewis had gone to meet Elard, leaving Mason and Elijah alone in the house.

The shop door would open at ten, but for today, that wasn't their problem. Lewis had offered to look after her for a few days to give them time to adjust to their new reality.

"No one asked us if this was what we wanted." Elijah wrapped his arms around Mason from behind. He'd been very quiet after breakfast, and disappeared into the back garden for a while, supposedly to give Mason and Lewis some time to get acquainted.

"I think it is. What I want, I mean." Mason spoke slowly, measuring his words, trying them out aloud. "We could do a lot of good and make a real difference to people's lives. I like the idea of providing a safe haven, a place to retreat from life for a few hours, and being there to listen to people who have no one else to talk to. We both have extra abilities we could use to help them find their way. I don't know about you, but I can't go back to data entry."

"We both figured Postscript had the potential to do some good." Elijah rested his head on Mason's shoulder. "Neither of us signed up for all this magical shit, though."

"We don't have to stay for decades like they did." Mason leaned into Elijah. "If we do this, it has to be because we both want to. If you have any doubts, I won't do it alone."

"You heard what Cyrus said. She needs two caretakers, one supernatural and one psi." Elijah grew quiet. "She's been good to you, this place. You came to Kedgetown because of Lewis, but I can see the difference in you. You're more confident in your ability, and you're excited about living again."

Mason turned in Elijah's arms. "That wasn't just Postscript. You gave me the spark I was lacking. I meant what I said about you being home." He kissed Elijah then studied him. "I want to give this a go, but I'll walk away with you if you don't want to stay."

"I had a long talk with Cyrus while you and Lewis were bonding." Elijah bit his lip. "I do have reservations, but you're right. A lot of that is because this is magic. Or advanced science. Or whatever. We could do some good here. We were both excited to open the shop."

"Yeah, but we hadn't signed up to spend months of every year stuck in a pocket universe," Mason reminded him.

"We've talked about the difference in our lifespans. Doing

this means we could have more time together." Elijah leaned his forehead against Mason's. "I asked about the full moon too. I wouldn't risk being here with you like that."

"And?"

"During the months the shop is open, I'm a wolf during the full moon, but I'm still me, but I stay in wolf form the days either side of it too. It's a small price to pay. If she's closed, I don't have to turn under a full moon. Same way Cyrus wasn't contagious in the pocket universe on his anniversary, which is why Lewis is still human." Elijah flinched. "Although being a vampire with PTSD isn't something I'd wish on anyone. They had to get to this point anyway, which wouldn't have happened if they hadn't taken on the shop and everything that goes with it."

If Mason and Elijah didn't stay, Lewis and Cyrus couldn't leave. Someone would have to be found to take over when it was their turn.

"Postscript finds her new caretakers when they're needed. Lewis left me the house after he talked to Fiona last Christmas. I was struggling. I came to Kedgetown to find him but found you first."

"And I found you." Elijah met Mason's gaze. "I figure we owe Postscript, but not only that, I'd like to see if we can make a difference to those who pass through her doors. Let's give it a year, and if it doesn't work out, she'll find someone else, right? I don't want to turn it down and then realise six months from now that I've made a huge mistake. We wanted the bookshop, right?"

"You're sure?"

"Yeah, I am." Elijah brushed Mason's hair from his eyes. "I love you. Let's make this work. And if we're still here next year, I want to get married." He grinned. "If we can survive months together in a pocket universe with only each other for company, it must be true love."

Mason laughed. "Idiot. I love you too."

Wordsworth purred loudly, jumped off the sofa, and rubbed up against their legs. Lewis and Cyrus intended to travel once they'd left Postscript, which was no life for a cat, so Wordsworth would adopt the new caretakers as his own. He stared up at both of them, a smug expression on his face, even for a cat.

"Do you think?" Mason glanced at the cat, then at Elijah.

"That he knew we'd say yes." Elijah shook his head. "Of course not. He's only a cat, right."

"A magical bookshop cat and the oldest feline in the world."

"That painting is amazing." Fiona took a step back to take a better look. "I love how the landscape feels like it goes on forever, yet still has a sense of home. It gives me the same feeling the shop does."

"Like coming home." Mason had finished the painting the night before and hung it that morning before they'd opened. He'd kept his original sketch for Lewis and Cyrus, certain they'd see each other again. That way, although they'd left the shop, they'd still have a tangible reminder of the pocket universe they'd inhabited for so long.

"That's Wordsworth under the mānuka tree by the edge of the stream, right?"

"Of course." Mason grinned. "The painting wouldn't be complete without him."

Fiona laughed. "That cat has you wrapped around his paw already."

"He takes his duties very seriously."

"It's good to see you painting again. I was worried when you didn't for so long." Fiona watched Elijah interact with a couple of the customers. She leaned in and lowered her voice. "He's cute, and he makes you happy. I hoped you and this town would be good for one another, but finding Elijah? Even better."

Mason wasn't about to tell his sister that Elijah could hear their conversation with his werewolf hearing. Not only that, but there was at least one other vampire and werewolf in the shop. He'd been practising figuring out what their customers were, and Elijah showed him the tells to look for.

"You're still coming for Christmas dinner tomorrow?"

Mason didn't want to lose contact with her like Lewis had with Nana. Mason had told her he and Elijah would be out of contact while the shop was closed, but not why. Lewis and Fiona had talked a little about Postscript so she wouldn't worry about Mason. She didn't need to know about supernaturals yet, and he'd know when the time was right.

"Wouldn't miss it." Fiona gave him a wink. "Besides, it's a great opportunity to get to know my potential brother-in-law better, right?'

Elijah turned and raised an eyebrow.

"You're jumping the gun a bit there, Fi." Mason shoulder-bumped her. "But you'll be the first to know when we get that far."

She grinned. "When, not if, hmm?"

Mason didn't bother correcting her. He and Elijah had enjoyed nearly two months of running Postscript together. A couple of days after the shop had reopened, Lewis and Cyrus had vanished, returning to the 1940s.

The keys hadn't reappeared, either. Lewis had figured they only appeared when the shop was closed if the care-takers were about to change. He'd also theorised that they held the spirits of the current caretakers, although Mason and Elijah agreed not to dwell on that idea. Having a good-sized pocket universe to explore sounded much less creepy.

Only caretakers, or those invited by them, could enter the

shop during the months it was closed. Anyone trying to break in walked through the door only to find themselves back where they'd started.

Once the shop closed again, they'd also have access to the journals of previous caretakers. Cyrus said they were interesting reading as the shop had been there almost as long as the town and suggested checking out the journals connected to the first world war.

"It's been great to finally meet you." Elijah wandered over, saving Mason from answering Fiona. "I'm looking forward to catching up over Christmas. You don't live that far away, so don't be a stranger."

"Thanks. You've both done an amazing job with the shop. It looks great, and it's buzzing today." Fiona glanced behind her, then smiled. "I'm going to go talk to your Aunt Rilla before I head home. I'll come say goodbye before I leave." She paused. "I'm checking out the bakery first. After all your talk of it, I need to take home some goodies."

Rilla waved from the doorway.

"Later!" Fiona returned the wave and walked over to meet her.

"That's going to be trouble." Elijah watched them go. "Rilla loves your sister."

"Tell me about it. They're going to encourage each other." Mason chuckled. "Until Rilla decides Fiona needs to find her special someone."

"That's not a bad thing." Elijah stole a brief kiss. "I'm going to clear tables and start the dishwasher. Yell if you need me."

"Yeah, I will. Or I'll ring the bell." Mason loved the old-fashioned bell on the counter. Cyrus and Lewis had given it to them as a shop warming present.

Elijah grabbed a tray and headed for the tables. Wordsworth was stretched out on the windowsill of the large bay window, enjoying the sun. He still looked for Lewis on occasion but, on the whole, had settled into life with his new charges. He was an affectionate cat and alternated laps in the evenings while they read or watched TV.

He especially loved Elijah in his wolf form. Last full moon, the two of them had stretched out in the sun in the shop and gone to sleep. Their human customers had thought Elijah was a large dog and commented on his friendship with the bookshop cat. Postscript's magic had a habit of showing people what they needed to see, and protecting its supernatural secrets was part of that.

Elijah spoke to the customers at the table closest to the door, then indicated the counter. Two of the three men were the new supernatural councillors. Mason had only exchanged a few words with them, but they seemed nice enough, and he hadn't let on he knew who they were. If the council didn't know about psi or the shop, he had no intention of changing that.

One of the men said something in a low voice, then grinned when the vampire in their group rolled his eyes. The dark-haired man kissed the vampire on the cheek, then got up and approached the counter.

"Hi, I'm Ben." He held out his hand. "Elijah said you have a mail order service, so I was hoping I could sign up. I love your book selection, and I'd prefer to buy local and support you guys. You have a great selection of graphic novels, too."

Mason shook his hand. "Nice to meet you, and we appreciate that. I'm Mason." He reached under the counter and handed Ben a clipboard. "Our service is available during the months we're open. If you fill this form in, I'll add you to the list."

"Halloween to February, right?" Ben wrote down his contact details. "I'll do a bigger order with that in mind, then.

And it will be a good excuse to come collect them instead of you posting them out, if that works too."

"We like seeing our customers. The mail order is more for people who can't get here, but we're happy either way. Don't forget to visit Featherston while you're over here." Mason had made some contacts with the bookshop town, and they sent each other potential customers. "They have a great selection of other specialist bookshops."

"Simon's already onto that. He loves old books." Ben grinned. "Thanks. Is it okay if I get a coffee refill and park myself at our table while he and Josh attend a meeting? I don't want to hog space if you need it for other customers." He'd bought a stash of graphic novels and some MM paranormal romance books, which had amused his vampire husband.

"That's fine. Stay as long as you need."

Another hour and their customers would start heading home. Postscript stayed open later, leading up to Christmas. The time of year could be lonely for many, and finding somewhere they could forget their troubles for a while was a welcome haven.

The door opened. Mason glanced up, ready to greet new customers.

The two men paused in the doorway to take in their surroundings. Lewis waved and made his way to the counter. "This looks and feels amazing. You've done so much since we left."

Mason reached for the bell to let Elijah know, but he was already heading back into the shop. "Lewis!" Mason walked out from behind the counter to give his great-great uncle a hug. "How are you?"

"We were hoping we could join you for Christmas dinner." Cyrus watched them with a smile. "If we wouldn't be imposing, that is. We've only recently returned to New Zealand."

"Of course." Mason stepped back from Lewis and shook Cyrus's hand. "How were your travels?"

"We've seen so much." Lewis showed a hint of fang, a subtle confirmation of why he still looked the same as the last time they'd met. Eighty years had passed for them, although only a couple of months for Mason and Elijah. "We started our travels in Ireland, so Cyrus could show me his hometown, and we've moved around ever since, apart from spending a few years in places we liked."

Cyrus put his arm around Lewis's waist. "We're heading to Invercargill in a few days to visit Louisa's grave," he said quietly.

"My sister's in town too," Mason told them.

"It will be lovely to see her again." Cyrus gave a nod of approval at the selection of lemon-flavoured baking available with Postscript's coffee and tea selection. "And I need to talk to Mac and Adam."

Adam had never shared with anyone what had happened to him during the war or why he'd taken so long to come home. He'd tell his story when he was ready and not before. Postscript worked her magic at the right time for each person they helped. Mason had already learnt the hard way that she couldn't be rushed.

"We can stay with your aunts at their boarding house for the few days we're here," Lewis added.

"You're welcome to the couch." Elijah offered the arrangement they'd used when Postscript had reopened.

"Thank you, but the shop is busy this time of year, and you need your privacy." Cyrus brushed the hair from Lewis's eyes, the gesture reminding Mason of Elijah. "Seeing Postscript confirms she has chosen well."

Lewis nodded. "She's content, and the two of you are

happy here." His gaze lingered on them as though seeing something others couldn't.

"You'll come back again, right?" Elijah asked the question before Mason could.

"You'll always be welcome," Mason added.

"Thank you, but no." Lewis slipped his hand into Cyrus's. "Postscript is your present and future, but she is our past. She gave us a gift for which we will always be grateful, but this visit is to tie up loose ends in Kedgetown, and say goodbye."

"Postscript is in your hands now." Cyrus smiled. "Take good care of her, and she'll look after you."

Mason put his arm around Elijah, holding him close. "She's already brought me my heart's desire and so much more."

ABOUT THE AUTHOR

CONNECT WITH ANNE
Contact me at:
annebarwell.wordpress.com
darthanne@gmail.com

Anne Barwell lives in Wellington, New Zealand. She shares her home with kitty siblings Byron and Marigold who are convinced her office chair is theirs.

In 2008, Anne completed her conjoint BA in English Literature and Music/Bachelor of Teaching. She has worked as a music teacher, a primary school teacher, and now works in a library. She is a member of the Upper Hutt Science Fiction Club and plays violin for Hutt Valley Orchestra.

She is an avid reader across a wide range of genres and a watcher of far too many TV series and movies, although it can be argued that there is no such thing as "too many." These, of course, are best enjoyed with a decent cup of tea and further the continuing argument that the concept of "spare time" is really just a myth. She also hosts and reviews for other authors, and writes monthly blog posts for Love Bytes. She is the co-founder of the New Zealand Rainbow Romance writers, and a member of RWNZ.

Anne's books have received honourable mentions five times, reached the finals four times—one of which was for best gay book—and been a runner up in the Rainbow Awards. She has also been nominated three times in the Goodreads M/M Romance Reader's Choice Awards—twice for Best Fantasy, once for Best Historical, and once for All-Time Favourite M/M Author.

Double Exposure

Vampires and werewolves live long lives. *The Sleepless City* saga might have ended but the story continues…

Someone is hunting supernaturals.

Vampire Simon Hawthorne and his human partner Ben Leyton's plans for a peaceful holiday with family are hijacked by the New Zealand Supernatural Council.

Tensions are on the rise in Wellington. Supernatural councillors are disappearing. Werewolves are suspicious of anyone human or vampire. If they don't work together, their enemy has already won.

And no one with a connection to the supernatural world is safe.